rhcbooks.com

ISBN 978-0-7364-3762-2 (hardcover)
ISBN 978-0-7364-3763-9 (paperback)

Printed in the United States of America
10 9 8 7 6 5 4 3 2 1

The Deluxe Junior Novelization

Adapted by **Suzanne Francis**

Random House 🏠 New York

Chapter 1

For six years, Wreck-It Ralph and Vanellope von Schweetz had been the best of friends. Every day, they worked as characters inside arcade games at Litwak's Family Fun Center and Arcade. Ralph played the Bad Guy in *Fix-It Felix Jr.,* while Vanellope raced go-karts in a game called *Sugar Rush.* But each evening, after all the players had left and Mr. Litwak had closed the arcade, Vanellope and Ralph left their games behind and met up in Game Central Station. They would spend the rest of their time hanging out and goofing around together.

One night, as the two sat on their favorite bench, they played a different kind of game while other characters walked by.

"Okay, I spy with my little eye . . . something

yellow and round, and . . . it eats dots," said Ralph.

"Seriously, Ralph?" said Vanellope.

"Of course I'm serious."

Vanellope knew exactly which character he was referring to.

"Why is that obvious?" Ralph asked.

Vanellope shook her head, amazed by Ralph's thought process.

Ralph and Vanellope hopped off the bench and walked through Game Central Station, making their way over to their favorite restaurant. Moments later, they were guzzling down soda at the counter, chatting about random things.

"Then he's like, 'Stop stealing my food, Ralph.' And I go, '*Your* food? I don't see your name anywhere on these chili dogs.'"

"But *were* they his chili dogs?" asked Vanellope.

"Of course they were his chili dogs," Ralph said.

After finishing their sweet drinks, the friends rode the train over to another video game. Along the way, they played rock, paper, scissors. On "shoot," Vanellope made the scissors sign and Ralph held out both pinkies.

"What is that?" asked Vanellope.

"Pinky lasers," said Ralph. "And pinky lasers destroy rock, paper, and scissors every time." Ralph pretended to fire his imaginary lasers. *"Pew-pew-pew-pew.* You lose."

"You're a loser," joked Vanellope.

"Nicest thing you ever said to me," Ralph declared with a smile.

Once they got to the video game, Ralph and Vanellope continued to goof off. The game was set inside a swamp, and there were lots of logs for them to roll on.

"Abandon ship! Man overboard!" shouted Vanellope. She laughed as she jumped to a nearby log, causing Ralph to flail and plunge face-first into the swamp.

Later, Ralph and Vanellope went for a visit inside a football game.

"Do you realize we're basically just zeroes and ones floating around the universe like tiny specks of dust?" asked Vanellope. Ralph and Vanellope looked up at the sky as they hung out on the fifty-yard line, tossing a football back and forth. "Like, doesn't the very nature of our existence make you wonder if there's more to life than this?"

"Why would I wonder if there's more to life when the life I got is perfect?" replied Ralph. For a moment, he thought back to before he met Vanellope, when he was wrecking buildings in *Fix-It Felix Jr.* and had no friends. "I mean, sure, it doesn't look so hot on paper. Y'know, I *am* just a Bad Guy who wrecks a building. And, yes, for twenty-seven years, I basically lived like a dirty bum without any friends . . . but now I got a best friend who just happens to be the coolest girl in this whole arcade."

Vanellope smiled. "Aww, thanks, pal."

Ralph punched the ball with his giant fist and it flew through the goalposts. "Home run!" he cheered. Then he turned to Vanellope. "Let's go watch the sunrise."

As the sun began to peek over the horizon behind Litwak's, Vanellope and Ralph sat in Game Central Station, watching its light through an open socket, just like they did every morning.

"So you're saying there's not one single, solitary thing about your life that you would change?" asked Vanellope, still thinking about what Ralph had said on the football field.

"Not one. It's flawless," answered Ralph. "Think about it—you and me get to goof off all night long. Litwak shows up. We go to work. The arcade closes. Then we get to do it all over again. Only thing I *might* do different in that scenario would be not having to go to work. Other than that, I wouldn't change a thing." Just then, the outside light disappeared. "Hey, where'd our sunrise go?"

BEEP! BEEP! BEEP! A loud alarm blared. Litwak had just plugged something into the last remaining outlet in the power strip close to where Ralph and Vanellope sat.

Vanellope gasped. "That's the plug-in alert. Let's go see what it is!"

Chapter 2

Inside the arcade, Mr. Litwak stretched awkwardly as he bent to plug a new cord into the power strip.

A burst of excitement rushed through Game Central Station as the video-game characters began to chatter. Everyone was eager to see what the new game was. They all dashed toward the plug to try to catch a glimpse.

"Hey, Felix, Calhoun—whadda we got gettin' plugged in here?" Ralph asked.

"Well, Sonic thinks it's going to be a new pinball machine," Felix said. Then he turned to Calhoun. "What do you think, ladylove?"

"I bet you a shiny nickel it's a photo booth," Calhoun replied.

"Please be a racing game, please be a racing game," chanted Vanellope.

Everyone watched as the marquee above the plug finally lit up: WI-FI.

Ralph read the word aloud: "'Whiffee? Wifey?'"

A hedgehog from a video game smiled at Ralph. "It's actually pronounced 'Why-Fie,' Ralph," he said.

"I know," Ralph said defensively.

"And Wi-Fi is the Internet," continued the kind hedgehog. "Which I've heard is an online community where human beings go to shop and play games and socialize. It's said to be a wondrous, miraculous place."

"Fun!" Vanellope said.

Surge Protector stepped up with a stern look on his face, capturing everyone's attention. "Oh, no, it is not. That sign right there says 'Wi-Fi.' What it *should* say is 'DIE-Fi.'" Surge paused, waiting for the crowd to laugh, but everyone was silent. "Take the joke, guys," he said. "But really, the Internet is nothing to laugh at. It is new and it is different; therefore, we should fear it. So keep out. And get to work. The arcade's about to open."

Vanellope and Ralph lingered a bit as the crowd dispersed. "Figures," Vanellope said with a sigh. "We finally get something new plugged in and we're not even allowed to go there."

"Totally not fair," said Ralph.

"A new racing game would have been cool," she said with a shrug.

"Something wrong with your game?" asked Ralph.

"No," said Vanellope. "It's just—every bonus level's been unlocked. I know every shortcut. I'd kill for a new track."

"New track?" said Ralph. "You've already got three options."

"Yeah, I know. But don't you ever wish something new and different would happen in your game?"

"No," he answered immediately. He didn't even have to think about it.

"Well, agree to disagree," said Vanellope.

"I don't want to disagree," said Ralph.

"No, it's just something you say to end an argument."

"We're arguing? I don't wanna argue."

"Relax, relax. You're making it worse. Go to

work. I'll see you tonight, dung merchant," said Vanellope, turning away.

"All right," said Ralph. They both walked off toward their games, but then Ralph looked back, thinking about what Vanellope had said. "She wants a new track—she'll get a new track." Ralph smiled as a great plan fell right into his brain. He knew just what to do.

Chapter 3

Later that day, a girl named Swati and her friends were playing in the arcade at Litwak's. Swati put a few quarters into *Sugar Rush* and sat in the driver's seat. Her friend Nafisa watched as she prepared to play.

"Pick Vanellope," Nafisa said. "She's got the best super power."

"Yeah, the glitch," said Swati. "I love her."

Inside *Sugar Rush,* Vanellope's name was plastered all over the leaderboard. It seemed she won every time!

Vanellope sat in her car at the starting line along with Taffyta and the other racers. The *Sugar Rush* announcer's voice spoke up as the girls prepared to compete: "Drivers, start your engines."

"You're gonna lose today, princess," said Taffyta, giving Vanellope a nasty look.

"While I am technically a princess, Taffyta, I'd rather you just think of me as Vanellope—the racer who's about to kick your butt," said Vanellope.

The announcer spoke again, ending their conversation. "Three, two, one . . . GOOOOOOO!"

The racers hit their pedals and were off! Taffyta took the lead as Vanellope glitched her way through traffic, disappearing and reappearing farther and farther ahead of the rest of the pack.

"Scuse me, pardon me, coming through," Vanellope said as she passed one racer after another with ease. When she approached the Gumball Challenge, everything happened as usual. Huge gumballs rolled down a steep hill straight for her, but because she knew the track inside and out, it wasn't challenging at all. "One, two, and three gumballs." She effortlessly made her way around each one.

Taffyta still had the lead, but Vanellope easily caught up. When Taffyta spotted her, Vanellope leaned back in her seat and snored loudly. Then she perked up and said, "I'm sorry. I must have fallen asleep. Am I winning?" With a grin, Vanellope blasted past Taffyta.

Taffyta wailed as she fell to second place.

Vanellope safely rounded a turn out of the Gumball Challenge.

"And that's Vanellope with a huge lead!" said the announcer. "No one's gonna catch her now!"

In the meantime, Ralph, hidden away in the distance, was working on a new track. "Here she comes," he said to himself excitedly. "She's gonna love this. Right on time."

Soon Vanellope noticed three billboards.

The first one read LOOKING FOR SOMETHING NEW?

The second said AND DIFFERENT?

And finally: THEN TAKE THIS TRACK. . . .

Vanellope smiled as she read each one. She knew right away it was the handiwork of her best friend. "Ralph, you old son of a gun!" she said gleefully. "I'd say I've got time for a little detour." She steered her car toward the new track.

In the arcade, Swati noticed she was heading for something she'd never seen before. "Hey, look. I think I unlocked a new track!"

Vanellope went off-road onto Ralph's bumpy homemade track. There were candy-cane tree obstacles in unexpected places and super-dangerous jumps. As Vanellope went over the track, she howled with delight. "*Wa-hoo!* Thank you, Ralph!"

"You're welcome!" Ralph yelled, thrilled that Vanellope was enjoying his creation.

In the arcade, Nafisa urged Swati on. "Get back up there—you're going to lose!"

Swati yanked the wheel hard to the left, trying to get Vanellope back onto the regular track, but it wasn't working. "What's wrong with this thing?" she said, struggling to control the Vanellope racer. She pulled hard at the wheel again, and this time the whole thing came right off!

Vanellope rounded another turn and rocketed over the new track, hooting the entire way. "*Wa-hooooooo!*" She was having the time of her life . . . until suddenly, her tire hit a bump wrong, causing her to crash! Her car tumbled into a ditch and landed in a puddle of mud.

"Kid!" Ralph shouted, running to her. "Oh, man. I'm so sorry!" he said. "Are you okay?"

"Oh my gosh," Vanellope said. "That was so

much fun! What an amazing track! Thank you, thank you, thank you!" She hugged Ralph tightly, still exhilarated by the new course.

Ralph smiled and took his hero medal out from underneath his shirt. "You're welcome. You know I take my duty as your hero very seriously."

"You took a serious doodie *where?*" Vanellope joked.

Taffyta appeared on a hill above them with her hands on her hips. "Vanellope, get up here," she said in a serious tone. "We have a situation."

In the arcade, Swati held the steering wheel up apologetically to Mr. Litwak as other kids stood nearby watching her.

"Mr. Litwak, the Vanellope racer wasn't working, and I think maybe I turned the wheel too hard," Swati said. "I'm real sorry."

"Oh, it's okay, Swati," said Litwak, taking the steering wheel from her and stepping toward the game. "I think I can get it back on pretty easily."

Inside *Sugar Rush,* Vanellope and all the other racers stood around nervously talking to each other. Taffyta turned to Ralph. "What did you do?" she said angrily.

"He was just trying to make the game more exciting. Leave him alone," said Vanellope.

Ralph poked his head onto the game screen to see what was going on in the arcade. "Yeah, why don't you relax, Taffyta. Litwak will fix it."

"All right, on you go . . . ," said Mr. Litwak as he began to put the wheel back on the game. But when he tried to force it, the wheel broke—into two pieces!

"Um. Okay," said Ralph inside *Sugar Rush*. "Still not a problem. Obviously, he'll just order a new part."

Outside the game, Mr. Litwak's face fell. "Well, I'd order a new part," he said to the crowd of kids now gathered around, "but the company that made *Sugar Rush* went out of business years ago."

The kids were aghast.

"I'll try to find one on the Internet," said one kid, looking down at his phone.

All the kids dropped their heads as they began to do the same, searching their phones for a new steering wheel.

"Good luck," Mr. Litwak said. "That'll be like finding a needle in a—"

"I found one," said Swati cheerfully. "See, eBay has a wheel, Mr. Litwak." Swati held her phone up to show him.

"Really? Great," he said.

"See?" said Ralph inside the game. "Those kids have it under control."

Mr. Litwak adjusted his glasses as he read the information about the steering wheel on the phone. "Are you kidding me?" he scoffed. "*How* much? That's more than this game makes in a year." Mr. Litwak sighed. "I hate to say it, but my salvage guy is coming on Friday, and it might be time to sell *Sugar Rush* for parts."

The kids groaned as Mr. Litwak headed around to the back of the machine.

Ralph's eyes popped. "Litwak's gonna unplug your game!" he shouted. "Go. Run, run, run!" Ralph, Vanellope, and everyone else hurried out as chaos filled *Sugar Rush*.

Mr. Litwak yanked on the plug, trying to remove it.

Out in Game Central Station, Surge Protector was whistling to himself when suddenly the stampede of *Sugar Rush* characters tumbled out, filling the station in a flash.

"Gangway!" a couple of donut cops named Winchell and Duncan shouted as they trampled over Surge.

"What are you doing out of your game, for Peter's sake?" asked Surge, shocked and confused. "The arcade's open!"

"*Sugar Rush* is getting unplugged," Ralph explained.

Stressed *Sugar Rush* citizens continued to run every which way as Mr. Litwak jiggled the plug to get it out of the socket.

"We're homeless!" cried the donut cops.

"Calm down! Calm down!" said Surge, trying to collect himself.

"Oh, jeez. I'm freaking out hard," said Sour Bill, who, even when panicked, spoke in a low, deadpan voice.

"I've never seen this many gameless characters!" said Surge.

Vanellope stepped up to Surge. "Where are we supposed to go?"

"Stay here, I guess, until the arcade closes," he said. "Then we'll figure out where the heck we're gonna put you."

Worry and fear filled Vanellope, and she began to glitch. Different parts of her started disappearing and then reappearing rapidly. She couldn't believe it. Her game was gone.

Chapter 4

Later that night, Vanellope sat on the rooftop inside *Fix-It Felix Jr.,* resting her chin in her hands and staring out into the dark, quiet arcade. It was depressing to see the *Sugar Rush* console sitting by the front door, waiting to be picked up by Mr. Litwak's salvage guy.

Ralph bumbled onto the roof carrying food and camping supplies. "Okay, here we go," he said cheerfully. "I raided Gene's fridge. Good news—he has pie! Oh, and I took a bunch of his pillows and junk. I'm thinking we can make a fort up here. Or a yurt. Or we could stack the pillows and make an igloo. A pillow igloo. A pigloo!" He began stacking pillows. "So whaddya think, kid? Fort, yurt, or the obvious best choice, pigloo?"

But Vanellope didn't respond. She continued to stare out at her game, sad and lost in thought. Finally, she said quietly, "I can't believe I don't have a game anymore. What am I gonna do all day?"

"Are you kidding?" said Ralph. "That's the best part. You sleep in, you do no work, then you hang out with me every night. I've literally just described paradise."

"But I loved my game," said Vanellope.

"Oh, come on," said Ralph. "You were just belly-aching about the tracks being too easy."

Vanellope looked up at her friend. "That doesn't mean I didn't love it. Sure, it was predictable, but still . . . I never really knew what might happen in a race. And it's that . . . it's that feeling—the not-knowing-what's-coming-next feeling—that's the stuff. That feels like life to me, and if I'm not a racer anymore . . . who am I?"

"You're my best friend," said Ralph.

"That's not enough," said Vanellope.

"Hey," said Ralph, wounded by her words.

"No, I just . . ." Vanellope started to glitch.

"Are you—are you okay?" asked Ralph, concerned.

"It's fine. I'm fine. It's nothing." Vanellope took

a few deep breaths and managed to stop glitching. "I'm sorry," she continued. "I know I'm being weird. I think maybe I just need to be alone right now." Vanellope hung her head and turned away.

"Oh," said Ralph. "Okay. I'll meet you over at our favorite restaurant in a little while." He watched helplessly as she walked away.

Down below, Felix and Calhoun's apartment was packed with *Sugar Rush* characters, as well as some characters from other games.

Felix addressed the group. "All right, we've found good homes for so many of our chums from *Sugar Rush*. And we're just hoping a few more of you will open your doors and your hearts to those in need."

Gene pointed at Sour Bill as he stirred his drink. "That large green olive will fit in nicely with my décor," he said.

"I'm a sour ball," said Sour Bill bluntly.

"Well, beggars can't be choosers, can they?" said Gene. "Come along, condiment." He gestured for Sour Bill to join him.

"Mmm-kay," said Sour Bill as he followed Gene out of the apartment.

"Marvelous," Felix replied. "That just leaves the

racers, ten spirited youngsters looking for a home." He knew Vanellope would stay with Ralph.

The *Sugar Rush* racers lined up against the wall.

"We're, like, adorable," Taffyta said in the most unconvincing way.

"So, any takers?" asked Felix. Silence fell across the room as the remaining characters averted their eyes. No one was willing to take the colorful racers. "Anyone?" he repeated.

Calhoun grabbed Felix's hand and smiled at him. "Felix, I know we've never really talked about a family before. . . ."

"I know," said Felix, understanding what Calhoun was suggesting. "And it does feel like the kind of thing you just jump into with both feet and nary a plan."

Just like that, they'd made their decision. Calhoun turned to the others and announced, "Felix and I will give them sanctuary!"

Surge Protector nearly spit up his drink. "Can I have a word with you two?"

Felix and Calhoun looked at each other and then followed Surge into the kitchen. He closed the blinds and turned to them dramatically. "I get it. You've been married six years; you're looking to spice things up. But trust me, this is the wrong kind of spice. Those things are basically feral."

Calhoun stepped up to face Surge. "Pardon me, sir, but those youngsters are lambs in need of two kind, caring shepherds."

"How hard can parenting be?" Felix asked. "You treat the child like your best friend, you give them everything they want, and you just love their little socks off. Right, Tammy?"

"Darn tootin'," said Calhoun.

They turned away from Surge and opened the kitchen door. Out in the living room, the kids had taken over, knocking over furniture and bouncing around.

Taffyta, irritated, held up a remote control. "Your dumb TV doesn't work, Mommy."

Felix and Calhoun looked at each other, suddenly uneasy about their decision.

Surge popped out. "I told you so. . . ." Then one of the kids threw a trophy across the room and struck him on the forehead. "Ow!"

"Eee-oh, boy," said Felix. At that moment, Felix and Calhoun realized they were entering a strange new world.

Later that night, Ralph sat alone at the counter in the restaurant with an empty stool beside him. "Hey—" he started to say to the waiter.

"No, Ralph," the waiter interrupted. "I haven't seen Vanellope. Not since the last time you asked, thirty seconds ago."

"Sorry," said Ralph. "I'm just worried about her. She's glitching like crazy and acting super insecure. And get this—she said being friends with me wasn't enough for her. I mean, that's crazy. I'm a great friend."

"Who's being insecure, Ralph?" asked the waiter. "Come on, the kid just loves her game. Give her a break."

Ralph sighed and nodded as the waiter walked off to help another customer.

Just then, the door opened and Felix entered. He

stepped up to the empty stool beside Ralph. "Is this seat taken?" he asked.

Ralph was surprised to see him. "Felix? Since when do you drink soda?"

"Oh," replied Felix, looking at the soda in front of him. "Since tonight."

"I hear that. This one was supposed to be for Vanellope," said Ralph, nodding to the soda. "I guess you can have it."

"Oh, thank you," said Felix. He took a sip and winced, nearly choking. "Smooth."

"Why do I have to screw everything up?" said Ralph with a sigh. "I mean, it figures, just when my life was finally perfect . . ."

"Mine too," said Felix. "But hey, now I'm a father of ten. Isn't that just a blessing?" Felix swung his head back as he chugged down the rest of his drink and coughed. "Eee-oh, boy!" he croaked, slamming the empty glass onto the counter.

Ralph turned to Felix. "Wait, what'd you say, Felix?"

Felix looked at Ralph, confused. "Um, isn't that just a blessing?" he repeated.

Ralph shook his head vigorously. "No, no, the weird sound thing."

"Eee-oh, boy?" asked Felix.

"Eee-oh, buh?" repeated Ralph as something in his brain began to click.

"Eee-oh?" said Felix.

"Eee-buh?" said Ralph.

"Eee-oh, boy," said Felix.

"Eee-oh, boy! EBoy! EBoy!" Ralph shouted.

"What're you getting at there, Ralph?" asked Felix, still lost.

Ralph was excited. "That kid out in the arcade said there was a steering wheel part in the Internet at something called eBoy, or . . ." He grabbed his head as he tried to remember. "No, it was eBay. That's it—eBay!" he exclaimed.

"Ralph, are you thinking about going to the Internet and finding that part?" asked Felix.

"Getting that part's the only thing that's gonna fix the game, and that's the only thing that's gonna make Vanellope happy again."

Felix smiled. "And if *Sugar Rush* is fixed, all those lovable scamps living in my house—and destroying my sanity—will have homes of their own again!"

Felix placed a hand on Ralph's shoulder. "Ralph, this is an important mission. A noble mission. I'll cover for you."

"Thanks, pal," said Ralph, heading for the exit.

"Ralph, what about your tab?" called the waiter. "You owe me for the soda."

"Oh, Felix is gonna cover for me," said Ralph. Then he turned to the crowd in the bar. "Felix is paying!"

The crowd cheered.

"Eee-oh, boy," said Felix.

Chapter 5

Ralph ran back into his video game, where he found Vanellope trying to build a go-kart out of bricks. She kicked it in frustration and the whole thing fell apart.

"Boo!" Ralph shouted.

He startled Vanellope so much that she jumped up and glitched. "Ralph! What is wrong with you?"

"Start churning butter and put on your church shoes, little sister, cause we're about to blast off!" said Ralph excitedly.

"What are you even talking about?" Vanellope asked.

"We're going to the Internet." Ralph told her he wanted to find the part so they could fix her game.

"Really?" said Vanellope, shocked. "Oh my gosh! Really?"

"Yeah, I probably should have just said, 'We're going to the Internet.' We're going to the Internet! C'mon!" The two friends ran off together, feeling more energized than they had since Vanellope's game was unplugged.

Moments later, they approached Surge in Game Central Station. Surge was stoically patrolling the barricaded Wi-Fi plug.

"Hey, Surge," said Ralph. "Are we glad to see you." Ralph made up a lie that there was trouble over at another game.

"Yeah, we saw some undesirables causing a real donnybrook over there," added Vanellope.

"Oh, heck, no. Not on my watch," said Surge. "Appreciate the tip."

Ralph and Vanellope quietly giggled as Surge dashed off. Then they snuck into the plug. "So all we gotta do is find this eBoy place," said Ralph.

"*eBay,*" Vanellope corrected him.

They hopped onto a moving sidewalk inside the router plug and chatted as they traveled upward.

"Right, eBay," said Ralph. "We go there, get the wheel, and have it delivered to Litwak before Friday. He fixes your game. Everything goes back to the way it was. Boom. Happily ever after."

"This is a shockingly sound, well-thought-out idea for you, Ralph," said Vanellope. "No offense."

"I know. And none taken."

The moving walkway neared its end and Ralph announced, "Ooh, here it comes. Ladies and gentlemen, boys and girls, I give you . . . the INTERNET!"

They entered the router and looked around, expecting to see something amazing. But the space around them was mostly empty. There really wasn't anything going on.

"Huh, the Internet is not nearly as impressive as how the hedgehog described it," said Ralph.

"Yeah. I gotta admit, I'm underwhelmed," agreed Vanellope. "I wonder where they keep their eBay."

"Hello, anybody home?" said Ralph.

"Hello!" called Vanellope. "We're looking for eBay!"

"Didja hear that?" asked Ralph. "Sweet echo. Listen, this'll be super cool." Then, he said as loudly as possible, *"Ka-kaw, ka-kaw!"*

Vanellope smiled and joined in the fun, calling, "*Hoo-lee-hoo! Hoo-lee-hoo!*"

Meanwhile, Mr. Litwak sat at his office desk, staring at his computer screen. He moved the mouse across the pad. "Okay, connect to network," he said, searching for the Wi-Fi icon on the menu bar. "Bingo. Password is HighSc0re, with a zero instead of an *O*. And we . . . are . . . online!" Mr. Litwak clicked on an icon. Suddenly, what appeared to be a little man who looked just like Mr. Litwak traveled at light speed from the computer to the Wi-Fi router. It was his avatar.

Ralph and Vanellope were still squawking like birds and enjoying their echo fun when a green light turned on nearby.

"Oh, Ralph, look!" said Vanellope.

"Whoa, cool," said Ralph. "Mood lighting."

Litwak's avatar appeared before them and Ralph screamed. "Aaaah! That's a gremlin! Stay away!"

"It looks like a tiny Mr. Litwak," said Vanellope.

The little Mr. Litwak avatar turned and moved down a platform.

"Come on, Ralph, let's follow him," Vanellope said, and ran after the tiny Litwak figure.

Ralph and Vanellope watched as Litwak's avatar was encased in a small capsule. A voice read out a computer address with some numbers, and the friends gazed in awe as the capsule suddenly blasted through a tube, zooming away.

Vanellope glitched onto the launch pad, ready to go after him, and Ralph followed. "Whoa!" said Vanellope as she was enclosed in a capsule of her own. "Cool!" Just like Litwak's avatar, she was catapulted into the net.

"Wait for me," said Ralph. "Come on, I want to go." He stepped up toward the launch pad but tripped and fell. Soon he was encapsulated, too, but because he was so big, his pod looked like it might burst. "Hey! I can't breathe!" Ralph screamed, but his voice was muffled by the tight fit.

Ralph and Vanellope flew like lightning through the cables. They were on their way to the Internet!

Chapter 6

"**R**alph!" cried Vanellope, thoroughly enjoying the wild ride. "Isn't this great?"

"No, it's not!" said Ralph, hating every second. The pod seemed to get tighter and tighter around his body, like it was strangling the life out of him.

When they finally stopped, they were released at the browser's home page.

"Sweet mother of monkey milk!" said Vanellope, landing on her feet. Her eyes widened as she looked around. Bright lights, skyscrapers, and crowds were everywhere. Vanellope was completely entranced. It was like nothing she had ever seen before.

Ralph splatted onto the floor, then slowly got up and looked around. "Holy cow. Kid, I don't think we're in Litwak's anymore."

"We most certainly are not, friendo. We are in the Internet! C'mon, Ralph!" Vanellope excitedly dashed off and Ralph followed. They reached an overlook and stood gazing down on millions of websites, awestruck. Each site looked like its own island city, and they were all connected by a floating, sprawling superhighway that stretched out in every direction as far as they could see. Avatars roamed in and out of the websites. The entire thing looked like a futuristic mall!

"Wow," said Ralph. "Look at all this stuff."

"This is the most beautiful miracle I've ever seen," said Vanellope.

"Yeah, it's really something," agreed Ralph.

"But it's too big. It goes on forever and ever," Vanellope said, nervously glitching. "How are we possibly gonna find eBay out there?"

"It's okay," Ralph said, trying to calm her. "Not to worry. I'm sure there's someone who can give us directions. Um . . ." Ralph looked around and noticed an egg-shaped character wearing glasses and a graduation cap. "Oh, that little egg guy has on one of those hats that smart people wear. Maybe he can help us."

KnowsMore, an upbeat, eager know-it-all, stood

behind a search bar. He lit up as users approached via their computers. "Welcome back to the search bar, madam," he said. "I hope you were able to find a satisfactory breakfast burrito based upon the search results I provided this morning. What can KnowsMore help you find now?"

On a quiet tree-lined street in suburbia, a woman sipped coffee as she stared at her computer screen. The letter *B* blinked as she began typing the word "ballet" on her keyboard. She spoke aloud as she typed, "Where can I find ballet—"

"Ballet shoes? Ballet classes? Ballet folklorico?" KnowsMore blurted, eagerly trying to guess the rest of her request.

"Ballet TIGHTS," said the woman as she continued to type. "Girls' size small," she added.

"Oh, little Madeline's trying ballet now, is she?" said KnowsMore. "I hope this lasts longer than the soccer phase."

The woman clicked the return button on her keyboard, and tons of results from KnowsMore's search popped up on the screen. "I found twenty-three million results for 'ballet tights, girls' size small,'" said KnowsMore.

As the woman clicked on one of the results, a pod formed around her avatar. A split second later, she was whisked off onto the information super-highway and taken to a specific website without so much as a word.

"They never say thank you," KnowsMore said to himself after she left.

As the woman departed, Ralph and Vanellope stepped up. "Oh, hello, sir," KnowsMore said to Ralph. "Welcome to the search bar. What can KnowsMore help you find today?"

"Um . . . ," Ralph said, trying to think of how to phrase his question.

"Umbrella," said KnowsMore, guessing Ralph's request. "Umbrage. Umami. Uma Thurman."

"No—" Ralph said, and he was interrupted again.

"Noah's Ark. No Doubt. Nordstrom Rack." KnowsMore continued shooting out guesses.

"Rrrrrgh," Ralph growled, frustrated.

"Ergonomics," continued KnowsMore. "Urban Outfitters. Urkel, played by Jaleel White."

"Looks like no one put Humpty Dumpty together again," said Ralph, leaning over to Vanellope. "This guy's a little soft-boiled."

"I'm pretty sure he's just trying to guess what you're gonna say," said Vanellope.

"Yes, I'm sorry. My autofill is a tad aggressive today," explained KnowsMore, embarrassed.

"Lemme try," said Vanellope. She typed in "eBay Sugar Rush steering wheel." She pushed the return button.

"Oh, I only found one result for your query. Hmm, isn't that interesting," said KnowsMore as a photo of the *Sugar Rush* steering wheel on sale at eBay popped up.

"How did you . . . ?" asked Ralph, dumbfounded.

"Oh, the Internet is very intuitive," said Vanellope with a grin. Then she clicked on the result. She and Ralph were instantly encased in a pod.

"Redirecting to eBay," said the robotic voice.

"Thank you, Mr. KnowsMore!" Vanellope shouted before they were whisked away.

"Oh, I *like* her," KnowsMore said. "What a delightful girl."

Vanellope and Ralph zipped along the super-highway. As the pod moved forward, Ralph and Vanellope stared wide-eyed through its translucent walls, gazing at all the sights.

They whipped by Google. "Guess we know where to go if we ever need goggles," said Ralph. "There's a whole building full of them."

"There it is!" screeched Vanellope, pointing out the sign. "eBay!"

The friends cheered, more than ready to get the steering wheel and save Vanellope's game.

Chapter 7

The pod dropped them off at eBay's plaza, where avatars and netizens rushed in every direction. Vanellope and Ralph tried to stay focused as they made their way toward the entrance, but a variety of pop-ups surrounded them, shouting out their advertisements and distracting Ralph.

"Get rid of belly fat using this one weird trick!" said one.

"Ooh, I like weird tricks," said Ralph.

"Sassy housewives want to meet you!" another pop-up said.

"They do?"

Before he could ask for more information, a pop-up was right in his face. "Congratulations—you're a winner!"

"Really?"

Another popped up and said, "These ten child stars went to prison. Number six will amaze you!"

"That sounds interesting," said Ralph.

A pop-up named Spamley appeared and asked, "You wanna get rich playing video games? Click here to find out how."

"For real?"

"Raa-alph, come on!" shouted Vanellope, eager to get to eBay.

"But there's a lot of cool stuff here," said Ralph.

"I'll be right here if you change your mind, brother," said Spamley. Then he turned his attention to another nearby avatar as Vanellope dragged Ralph away.

Vanellope and Ralph entered eBay to find a giant bazaar that looked like a flea market. Avatars stood at different counters, calling out bids as auctioneers rattled off numbers.

"Next up is a black velvet painting of a sorrowful kitten," said an auctioneer. "Bidding starts at twenty-five." The fuzzy feline painting hung behind him, staring out with oversized, sad eyes against a black velvet background.

At the next counter, another announcer stood by a stuffed beaver, calling, "Fifty for the beaver, the beautifully taxidermied beaver—"

Ralph and Vanellope walked slowly, taking it all in. Some people were even bidding on an artificial hip! Then the friends stopped to watch an auction for a potato chip in the shape of a celebrity.

"Fifty-fifty-fifty. Now, who will gimme two fifty?" barked the auctioneer.

"Four hundred!" shouted a bidder.

"Going-once-going-twice-and-sold!" shouted the auctioneer.

The winning bidder jumped up and down joyfully.

Ralph looked over at Vanellope, utterly confused. "Are you understanding how this game works?"

"I think all you have to do is yell out the biggest number and you win," replied Vanellope.

Ralph shook his head and told Vanellope it was the weirdest game he'd ever seen. He was focused, though, and told Vanellope to glitch up onto his shoulders. From there she had a better chance of spotting the steering wheel.

"Let's see, there's a bunch of sports memorabilia,"

Vanellope said, still searching. "Oh, there's a row full of old video-game junk!" She pointed excitedly. "There it is! I see it! Whoa, someone else is trying to win it. Hurry, let's go!"

With Vanellope still on his shoulders, Ralph raced through the crowd, knocking avatars out of the way. "Move!" he shouted.

A hologram of the *Sugar Rush* wheel appeared behind the auctioneer. A clock was ticking down, with only thirty-five seconds to go, and one avatar had already put in a bid!

"Two-and-two-and-two-and-two-and-two-seventy-five," said the auctioneer. "And with thirty seconds left in this auction, we have two seventy-five. Do I hear three-and-a-three-and-a-three-and-a-three?"

Ralph and Vanellope arrived, and Ralph blurted, "I'll give you three! Right here! Three!"

"I heard three, three, three, I heard three!" shouted the auctioneer.

"Three oh-five," said the other bidder.

"Three oh-five—who'll gimme three ten?" said the auctioneer.

"Three ten," said Ralph.

The other bidder offered 315, and Ralph offered 320. Then the bidder offered 325. Ralph leaned toward Vanellope and whispered, "Oh, man. This guy's good."

The auctioneer shouted, "I have three and a quarter. Do I hear three fifty?"

Vanellope elbowed Ralph and said, "Watch this." Then she shouted, "One thousand!"

"We now have a bid of one thousand," said the auctioneer.

"Smooth move!" said Ralph, impressed by Vanellope's skills. Vanellope thanked him, and then Ralph said, "Check this out." He eyed the auctioneer shrewdly and shouted, "Fifteen thousand!"

"Fifteen thousand. Do I hear fifteen-five?" said the auctioneer.

"Fifteen-fiver!" shouted Ralph, feeling like he was really getting the hang of it.

"Sixteen!" shouted Vanellope.

The two friends continued to shout out higher and higher numbers, enjoying the game, all the way up to twenty-seven. Just before the timer ran out,

Ralph made one last bid: "Twenty-seven and one!"

"And—sold!" shouted the auctioneer. "For twenty-seven thousand and one to the barefoot hobo in the broken overalls."

"Hey, that's me!" said Ralph, beaming with pride.

"We won!" cheered Vanellope.

"Congratulations. Here is your voucher," said the auctioneer, handing Ralph a slip of paper. "Please take it to checkout for processing."

Ralph and Vanellope exchanged a celebratory fist bump and headed off to the checkout area, victorious.

Chapter 8

Ralph and Vanellope arrived at the checkout and were greeted by a straight-faced clerk named Elaine.

"So," she said, looking over Ralph's voucher. "We are set to ship one *Sugar Rush* steering wheel to Litwak's Family Fun Center in Los Aburridos, California. With expedited shipping, that should arrive Wednesday morning."

"That's two whole days before Litwak scraps your game. We're way ahead of schedule," said Ralph.

"We rule," said Vanellope.

"I'll just need a credit card number," said Elaine.

"Sorry, what's a cacca-nummah?" asked Ralph.

"A credit card number, please," said Elaine, an impatient tone creeping into her voice.

Ralph and Vanellope exchanged a worried look. "Number," said Ralph. "Right. Uh, seven?"

Elaine frowned. "Excuse me?"

"Sorry, no—that's, you're right, that's ridiculous. I meant eleven," said Ralph.

"Those aren't credit card numbers," said Elaine, now very annoyed.

"I'm pretty sure they are," said Ralph.

Elaine narrowed her eyes at Ralph. "How exactly do you intend to pay for this item, sir? You owe twenty-seven thousand and one dollars."

Ralph was completely stunned.

"Dollars? Dollars, like money?" asked Vanellope.

"Yes, and if you don't have a credit card, we also accept PayPal, Venmo, ProPay, Square Cash, and BuzzzyBuxxx," explained Elaine.

"You're gonna laugh," said Vanellope. "Okay, so this big galoot, he left his wallet at home."

"Yeah, yeah, I did leave my wallet at home, in my wallet room," said Ralph, going with Vanellope's story. "And the door's locked."

"Look," said Elaine, tired of dealing with their ridiculous behavior. "If you don't pay within twenty-four hours, you will be in violation of the unpaid-item policy, you will forfeit the bid, and you will lose this item." Elaine leaned around them and shouted toward the line, "Next!"

Ralph and Vanellope walked away, both feeling disappointed, but Ralph was also fuming mad. He ranted to a passing avatar, "Hey, buddy, you going to eBay? Well, I got some free advice for you: don't. What a scam!" He tried to punch a sign that read BARGAIN OF THE DAY, but it was a hologram, so his giant fist just slipped right through it. "Look, their signs aren't even real!" he screamed. He yanked the sign out of the ground and hurled it as hard as he could. It crashed right into a nearby avatar and knocked her down.

In a studio apartment outside the Internet, a woman frowned at her computer screen, annoyed that she was just kicked off eBay. "What the heck. I was gonna bid on lipstick," she whined.

Feeling powerless, Ralph collapsed into a heap. Then he noticed Vanellope glitching worse than he'd ever seen before. He got up and rushed over to her. "Hey, come on, kid," he said gently. "What's going on? What's wrong?"

"This was our only chance and we blew it,"

Vanellope said. "There was only one wheel in the whole Internet, and we blew it. We blew it."

"Hey, calm down. We came here to save your game. That's what we're gonna do," Ralph said confidently.

Vanellope took a deep breath. "Okay . . . okay."

"There you go. See. All we gotta do is figure out a way to earn a little bit of moola."

"We're video-game characters, Ralph. We don't *have* moola. Unless you can think of some magical way to get rich playing video games."

They looked at each other—they suddenly remembered one of the pop-ups they had seen earlier: Spamley! They hurried off to find him.

"Wanna get rich playing video games! Click here to find out how," said Spamley to avatars as they passed him.

"Back off, pop-up!" said a pop-up blocker, punching Spamley and knocking him to the ground.

"Oof," said Spamley, brushing himself off. "Dang pop-up blockers. Why's everybody gotta be so mean?"

"Oh, there you are," said Ralph, walking up to him. "Thank goodness you're still here. Me and my friend here, we got twenty-four hours to make twenty-seven thousand and one dollars or she loses her game."

"Yeah, so, can you please tell us how to get rich playing video games?" asked Vanellope.

"You bet!" said Spamley, more than happy to help. "Come on, click right here. I'll take you to my website."

Ralph clicked, and he and Vanellope were encased in Spamley's strange, rickety pod, which had some trouble lifting off because of Ralph's size.

"You got an ample carriage there, buster," Spamley said. "Causing quite a drag."

As they rose up onto the superhighway, Spamley's pod headed toward a steep drop-off and Ralph panicked.

"You're getting close to the edge," he said. "You see that? That's the edge. That's the edge. Ahhh!"

The pod fell into the drop-off but managed to barely stay afloat as it continued on its way.

"By the way, my name is JP Spamley, and I'd like to welcome both of you to the Spamley family."

They landed minutes later, and Spamley led them to his site. Stacks of paper, garbage, and empty food containers were everywhere. It looked more like a hoarder's home than a professional workplace. Ralph and Vanellope recoiled from the rotten stench.

"So this is your website?" asked Ralph, feeling doubtful.

"I know what you're thinking, and it is a bit of a mess," Spamley said. Then he turned and shouted, "Hey, Gord!" He focused his attention back on them and continued, "But I do have a system here, if I could just find that list. . . ." He turned and shouted again. "GORD!"

Suddenly, a short, round guy in a brown chunky sweater appeared behind Ralph and Vanellope, startling them. Spamley told Gord that they were looking to make some money by playing video games, and Gord handed them each a stack of what looked like Wanted posters.

Ralph read each aloud as he looked at it. "'Fishwife's amulet, *Wizard Quest,* three dollars. Foxhole hammer, *Zombie Crusades,* five dollars.'"

"Now, those are some of your more common-place, low-dollar items," said Spamley.

"Can you back up a sec, Mr. Spamley?" asked Vanellope, reading one of her sheets. "You're saying if we find the golden cleats from *Pro League Soccer*— if we find those and bring them back here—then a human being in the real world will pay us fifteen dollars?"

"Yes, ma'am," answered Spamley.

"So this is a real thing?" asked Ralph. "People actually do this?"

"What're ya, soft in the head?" said Spamley with a chuckle. "Of course they do."

Ralph was completely shocked.

"Here's the thing," said Vanellope. "We need, like, a *buttload* of money. Do you have any more lucrative items, perchance?"

"GORD!" shouted Spamley. Gord appeared and handed over another sheet of paper. "Is forty thousand dollars lucrative enough for you?" asked Spamley.

"It's more than enough!" exclaimed Ralph.

"Then all's you gotta do is bring me Shank's car from a game called *Slaughter Race*."

Ralph and Vanellope exchanged a look of excited disbelief. "Wait, a racing game?" said Vanellope.

"That's right," said Spamley. "*Slaughter Race* is the most popular online racing game out there. However, it is wicked dangerous."

"Don't worry, the kid's the best racer in the world," said Ralph. "We'll get you that car, no problemo."

Feeling hopeful again, Ralph and Vanellope hurried over to *Slaughter Race*.

Chapter 9

Moments later, Ralph and Vanellope walked through *Slaughter Race*. A car exploded beside them and Vanellope smiled, giddy. "Okay, this game is kind of amazing," she said, looking around.

"Yeah, the attention to detail is impressive. I've never been to a game with smog," said Ralph, feeling a little uneasy. A ferocious-looking dog appeared, growling and baring its teeth. "Ahhh!" screamed Ralph. "Nice kitty . . ."

"Easy, boy," said Vanellope as they slowly backed up. "Easy . . ."

The dog lunged at Ralph, but just before it reached him, a great white shark emerged from the sewer and chomped down! Just like that, their dog problem was solved, and the shark quickly retreated back into the sewer.

Ralph breathed a huge sigh of relief. "Let's just find Shank's car and get outta here," he said.

"Agreed," said Vanellope, nodding.

Ralph and Vanellope found a warehouse and climbed up onto an outside ledge. They snuck inside through a broken window and surveyed from above. Down below, they could see Shank's car!

"Whoa," said Vanellope admiringly. "That car is gorgeous. No wonder it's worth so much."

But before Ralph and Vanellope could make a move, avatars for two players crept into the warehouse.

One of the players, Jimmy, sat in his bedroom, while the other player, Tiffany, was in her living room.

"Thirty-one hours of continuous game play, and we've finally found Shank's car," Jimmy said into his headset. "Come on, let's jack this ride."

"Oh, it's on," said Tiffany.

Jimmy's grandmother called to him from downstairs, "Jim! Jimmy? You're not playing that horrible game again, are you?"

"No, Gramma, I'm doing my homework," he answered. Then he whispered into his headset. "Okay, like I was saying . . . let's jack this ride."

Inside the game, the two players headed toward Shank's car.

A group of scary-looking characters in the warehouse surrounded Jimmy and Tiffany threateningly. Shank sauntered in like it was no big deal, keeping her cool.

"Well, well, well," she said. "While the cat was away, these mice tried to play."

"Hey," whispered Ralph, "I think that might be Shank."

"Listen up, *mice:* anyone who tries to play with this cat's ride is gonna get *got,*" said Shank.

"You're going down, Shank," Jimmy said, pulling out a board with nails in it.

"Pyro," ordered Shank. "Give these punks the works."

Pyro, a member of Shank's crew, pulled two flamethrowers off his back and dramatically ignited them. Then he narrowed his eyes and approached the avatars with his weapons.

In an instant, END OF THE ROAD appeared on

Jimmy's screen in his bedroom over a burned image of his avatar and Tiffany's.

"Aw, gosh dangit!" said Jimmy. "Now we gotta start all over."

Ralph immediately turned to leave and Vanellope asked him where he was going.

"I'm scared," said Ralph. "If we get burned up in here, we're dead, we're gone. So I think we should get out of here right now."

Vanellope stopped him. "I have an idea." She led Ralph to another area of the warehouse.

With the avatars gone, Shank and her gang hung out discussing their game. Pyro turned to Shank and asked thoughtfully, "Do you ever reckon we're going too hard on the players?"

"I have felt that way before," admitted Shank. "But the way I look at it, making life difficult for the players—that's our calling. It's why we're programmed the way we are."

Another crew member, named Felony, said, "Yeah, but to Pyro's point, I mean, those players worked so hard to get here."

"I hear you, Felony, but imagine a game without

challenges. The same predictable thing every single time—who would want that?"

"Shank's right," said Butcher Boy. "You know, I just saw a really insightful TED Talk, and I can't really remember what the guy said—it's more about how he made me feel—but I think, ultimately, the point was honor your journey, guys. . . ."

"And I honor you, Butcher Boy," said Shank sincerely.

Butcher Boy thanked her, and a girl named Debbie spoke up. "Hey, Shank. Didja ever wonder what it would be like if someone actually got your car?"

"Well, I know one thing—whoever does will have to be the best of the best," said Shank.

KNOCK! KNOCK! KNOCK! Suddenly, someone was banging on the warehouse door. Shank and the crew snapped to attention, grabbing their weapons and putting their game faces back on, ready to play.

Butcher Boy opened the door, revealing Ralph, gulping nervously.

"Good day to you, madam," Ralph said to Shank.

"Who are you?" asked Shank.

"I'm here from the, ah, Department of Noise? And the thing is, we've been getting some complaints down at HQ—uh, Larry's the one who takes the calls. . . ."

While Ralph distracted them, Vanellope tiptoed into the warehouse and hopped into Shank's car. "Whoa, this is nice," she said to herself. "Where have you been all my life?" She settled into the driver's seat as Ralph continued.

"Anyway, someone told Larry that we've been hearing a lot of gun sounds and screaming sounds and what-have-you. That sort of thing."

"Yeah, you mean the everyday sounds of this game?" said Shank. She took a step toward him and asked, "Who did you say you were again?"

"Oh, I'm . . . Larry?" said Ralph, failing miserably at his act.

"You said Larry took the call," said Shank.

Ralph stuttered as Vanellope stomped on the gas and headed straight for the *Slaughter Race* gang, forcing them to dive out of the way. Vanellope rammed the car into Ralph, plastering him to the hood as she sped off. Luckily, Ralph was so big that it didn't hurt him at all. He rolled into the passenger seat.

"Good job, Larry!" said Vanellope.

"Yeah, worked like a charm!" said Ralph.

The car blasted out of the warehouse, whipping past Jimmy's avatar, who had just appeared again in a brand-new car with Tiffany's avatar.

"Aw, someone got Shank's car," he said, envious.

Shank grabbed Jimmy's avatar by the neck and yanked him out. "And I need yours," she said as she hopped into the driver's seat.

"I'll just go," said Tiffany's avatar, jumping out and running off.

Back in his house, Jimmy threw his controller onto the floor. "This is the worst day of my life!" he shouted.

Jimmy's grandma called, "You having trouble with your algebra, Jim?"

Inside the game, Vanellope drove the stolen car down the highway. "It's a shame we have to leave so soon. This game is cool," she said, enjoying the thrill of driving through uncharted territory.

"Just get us out of here," said Ralph. He was not enjoying the ride.

"No problem," said Vanellope, focusing on the road.

But they were interrupted when Butcher Boy appeared out of nowhere and raced up behind them. "You mess with the bull, you get the horns!"

Vanellope pulled a slick move, causing Butcher Boy to crash into a wall. They thought they were in the clear, but then Ralph spotted Shank in Jimmy's car.

"Oh, no, it's that Shank lady," said Ralph. "She looks upset."

"Don't worry. I'll lose her," Vanellope said coolly. She took a curb and jumped off the road into a dry river basin.

"Where are you going?" yelled Ralph over all the commotion. "Kid, get back on the track. I'm gonna lose my cookies!"

"There is no track. I can drive anywhere!" Vanellope said gleefully. She hit the gas, turned the wheel, and disappeared into a tunnel.

Surprisingly, Shank stayed on their tail! "I believe you have something of mine," she said.

"Yeah, come and get it," taunted Vanellope. She spiraled around Shank and zipped out of the tunnel.

"This kid can drive," said Shank, impressed.

"Whoa, Mother Hubbard, this lady can really drive," said Vanellope. As hard as she tried to lose her, Shank was able to keep up.

Vanellope continued to expertly maneuver the car, but after making a turn, she found herself in trouble. She was about to crash into a huge pile of burning buses! The sight of the flames made Ralph scream.

"Kid, you see them. We're not gonna fit!" yelled Ralph, white-knuckling the dashboard. "Dead end! Dead end!"

Vanellope took a deep breath and grinned. "Not for me. Bye-bye, Shanky," she said, confident in her plan. She glitched right through the burning buses!

"Whoa! You got the glitch under control!" said Ralph, relieved.

"Yeah, cause I feel like me again! One exit, straight ahead!" cheered Vanellope.

"You're not gonna lose me that easy," said Shank, appearing next to them out of the blue.

Vanellope couldn't believe it! "Wha—? How did you—?"

"Uh, you might wanna keep your eyes on the road," said Shank. Then she revved her engine, drove up a loading ramp, and launched herself into the air. She landed directly in front of Vanellope. Ralph screamed as Vanellope spun out to avoid colliding with her. When they finally stopped, Shank and her crew stepped out of their cars and approached the two friends.

"Yo!" yelled Shank. "Department of Noise! Get out of my car."

Vanellope glitched as she and Ralph realized they were trapped, wondering what was going to happen next. They began to fear the worst.

Chapter 10

Ralph turned to Vanellope. "You just stay put. Don't panic. I'm gonna talk to her," he said.

"Ralph, be careful," said Vanellope, worried.

"It's fine. This is what heroes do." He started to get out of the car but realized he was stuck. He was squeezed in too tightly! He struggled, wiggling left and right, and finally managed to squeeze out of it. "Oof. That is not designed for a big boy," he muttered, getting up and dusting himself off.

"You guys thought you could just steal my car?" said Shank. "Let me tell you what's going to happen now—"

"Wait," said Ralph, interrupting her. "We aren't normally criminals. See, my friend here, she's a candy-kart racer. You should see her racing around her sweet little track in her cookie-wafer car that we built together. . . ."

Vanellope's gaze fell to the ground. She wished she could disappear while Ralph embarrassed her in front of Shank.

Shank looked at Vanellope and then back at Ralph. Tears filled Ralph's eyes.

"And the thing is," said Ralph, "her perfect little game broke." He was now wailing uncontrollably. "And that's partly on me, so we're here to fix it, but we need money to do that, and someone was gonna pay us money for your car, and—"

"Okay, okay, you can stop crying," Shank said, cutting him off. "Though I do respect your outward display of vulnerability."

"Thank you," said Ralph, trying to pull it together.

"Yeah, I mean, I get it. I do. Friendship is everything to us, too—right, guys?" Shank turned to her crew, and they all nodded in agreement.

"Word. We're like family," said Felony.

"I honor your journeys, guys," Butcher Boy said softly.

"That's really great," said Ralph. "So does this mean we can keep your car?"

"Absolutely not," said Shank. "But I do want to help. Felony, you got your phone on you?"

"You know it," replied Felony.

Shank told her to start recording and gestured for her to film Ralph. "Pyro, hit big boy with the blow-and-go," ordered Shank.

Before Ralph could react, Pyro started up a powerful leaf blower and pointed it directly at Ralph's face. The intense wind made Ralph's cheeks billow and shake as he screamed, "What are you doing?"

"Say something—first thing that comes to your mind!" yelled Shank.

"I'm gonna wreck it!" said Ralph.

"Good, good," said Shank. She turned to Pyro and told him to turn off the blower.

"What the heck did you do that for?" asked Vanellope.

"There are much better ways to make money on the Internet than stealing cars. Here," said Shank, taking the phone from Felony and handing it to Ralph. "Such as becoming a BuzzzTube star."

"Am I supposed to know what that means?" asked Ralph.

"I just started an account for you, Larry," Shank said. "Now lemme post the video." She clicked a few buttons on the phone. "There we are. If this thing goes viral, you can make a lot of money."

"Wait, for real?" Vanellope asked, surprised.

"Yeah. Friend of mine—chick named Yesss— she's the head algorithm over at BuzzzTube. Tell her I sent you. Yesss will hook you up."

"Wow," said Vanellope. "That's so nice of you."

"Not sure 'nice' is the right word," said Ralph, rubbing the pain from his cheeks.

"Thank you," said Vanellope.

"I should be thanking *you,* little sister. That race was fun," said Shank.

"Oh. Thank you. Again," Vanellope said, shocked to hear such high praise from Shank. "Um, say, while we're talking shop—what move did you do to get through those burning buses? Was it a power drift into a drift jump, maybe?"

"Maybe," said Shank coyly. "If you ever want to come back for a rematch, I'd be happy to kick your butt again." She jumped into her car, and Vanellope watched in awe as she zoomed away.

"Whoa," Vanellope said, admiring Shank's exit.

"Show-off," said Ralph, rolling his eyes. "C'mon, kid." He started walking away, but Vanellope wasn't following. He turned back to see her lingering inside *Slaughter Race*. Once they were outside it, he looked at her. "Man, that game is a freak show."

But she was bouncing with excitement. "I know!" she exclaimed. "I love freak shows, don't you?"

"No," Ralph said firmly.

"Come on—tell me that Shank lady wasn't the coolest person you've ever met," said Vanellope, still reeling from the game.

"Cool? Name one thing that's cool about her."

Vanellope quickly rattled off a list. "She looks cool. She talks cool. Her hair is cool. She drives cool. Her car is cool."

"Are you saying my hair isn't cool?" Ralph asked defensively.

Vanellope looked confused. "Wha—? No," she said, wondering why he was suddenly talking about himself. "I'm just sayin' that game was next level.

The racing was awesome—and there's no one telling you what to do or where to go."

Ralph and Vanellope reached an intersection, and while Ralph headed one way, Vanellope went the other. Ralph asked her where she was going.

"To BuzzzTube," she explained.

"No," Ralph said. "We're going back to Spamley's. He can give us some easier loot to find."

"What about Shank's algorithm friend?"

"Please," said Ralph sarcastically. "I don't trust Shank."

"Well, I do."

"Well—" But before Ralph could finish, a small boy appeared out of nowhere.

"Hello, mister," said the eBoy.

"Ah! Who are you?" Ralph asked.

"I'm your friendly eBay alert messenger," the eBoy said.

"Huh," Ralph said. "An actual eBoy."

The eBoy continued, "Just here to let you know your bid expires in eight hours."

"Eight hours?" Ralph gulped. There wasn't any time to waste. "Oh, man. Thanks, eBoy."

"You got it!" the eBoy said, disappearing as quickly as he'd arrived.

Vanellope looked at Ralph. "Chumbo, if we nickel-and-dime it with Spamley, it'll take us twenty years to make enough money."

Ralph considered what Vanellope was saying and sighed. He knew she wasn't wrong. "All right, fine," he said. "We'll do it your way. But I'm telling you right now, this BuzzzTube is a terrible idea."

Chapter 11

Moments later, Ralph and Vanellope entered the main floor of BuzzzTube. Thousands of random video clips appeared, floating before them.

"Who knew the world had so many babies and cats," Ralph said, trying to take it all in.

"Hey, look," Vanellope said, pointing to Ralph's video. "There's yours." They both watched as a netizen sucked up users' hearts with a big hose. A number measuring the amount had ticked up to 723,000.

"Why are they giving your video all those hearts?" Vanellope asked.

"Cause obviously they love me," he replied. "I toldja this place was a good idea."

"Doofus," said Vanellope with a giggle.

"Now, who are we s'posed to see about getting paid again?" asked Ralph.

"The head algorithm," Vanellope said. "Her name is Yesss."

Yesss sat in her office at her desk, frowning as she sifted through a stack of videos. Her assistant, Maybe, stood nearby. "NO!" she yelled. "NO. NO. NO! Uninspired, clichéd, YouTube's got this one. . . ." Suddenly, she stopped and pulled up a video so Maybe could see it. The video showed a man in a Chewbacca mask. "Chewbacca *Dad*? Really?"

"Yah, it's like Chewbacca Mom, but it's a daddy?" said Maybe cautiously.

"NO. I need next-level genius, not this drivel," said Yesss.

"Hey-o!" said Ralph, appearing in the doorway. Yesss peered over her sunglasses to see Ralph and Vanellope approaching. "Are you the head of Al Gore?"

"I am the head ALGOrithm of BuzzzTube, which means I curate the content at the Internet's most popular video-sharing site," explained Yesss. "Which means I don't have time to trifle with every shoeless mouth-breathing hobo that trundles into my office. Yo, Maybe, call security."

"Yes . . . But, Yesss," said Maybe, reaching for his phone, "he's the leaf-blower guy. His video has one point three million hearts."

"Well, that is different," Yesss said, completely changing her tone. "Why didn't you tell me I was in the presence of a genius?" Yesss got up and approached Ralph while Maybe brought him an iced beverage.

"Yeah, this lady named Shank told us to come see you," Vanellope said.

"*Slaughter Race* Shank? No wonder your video's so dope. Shank is for-real cool," Yesss said.

"Right?" said Vanellope. "She's like the coolest person I've ever met."

"*Pfft,* she is not," Ralph said. "I'm the cool one getting all the hearts from my famous video."

"That's right, baby," Yesss said. "What'd you say your name was?"

"Ralph. Wreck-It Ralph."

"Well, Wreck-It Ralph, you are trending! And these are for you," Yesss said. Then she began chanting, "Heart, heart, heart, heart, heart, heart, heart!"

Ralph was confused, but he joined in. "Heart, heart, heart, heart, heart!"

"Um, not to buzzkill the heart-fest," Vanellope said, "but Shank kinda told us that viral videos can make actual money?"

"Oh, hearts *are* money, honey. Here," Yesss said, handing Ralph and Vanellope each a Buzzzy device. "Your Buzzzy account converts hearts into dollars, see?"

Ralph looked at his account and saw the number forty-three. "Forty-three thousand dollars! We only needed twenty-seven thousand and one! Oh my gosh, kid. We did it!"

Yesss looked at Ralph. "That's forty-three dollars. As in, nowhere near twenty-seven thousand and one."

"But that's how much we need to save Vanellope's game," Ralph explained.

"And we only have eight hours left," Vanellope added, emphasizing their deadline.

"Oof, I hate to say it, but that ain't happening." Yesss looked at the phone. "In fact, your video's tapped out."

"Wait, I thought I was trenching?" Ralph said.

"Trending," Vanellope said, correcting him.

"You were, but that was fifteen seconds ago. Now you're not. Bye." Yesss turned and walked back toward her desk.

Ralph looked at Vanellope desperately. "What're we gonna do?"

"Calm down, pal," said Vanellope. "I bet if we asked really nice, Shank would let us take her car, or—"

"No," Ralph said immediately. He did not want to go back to Shank or anywhere near *Slaughter Race*. He stepped up to Yesss's desk. "What if you made a whole bunch of videos of me doing different things?"

"You mean saturate the market," Yesss said, thinking. "That could get you a lotta hearts fast."

"What exactly do you plan on doing in these videos?" Vanellope asked him.

"I'll just copy whatever's popular," he answered.

"Genius," said Yesss. "Yo, Maybe. What's trending right now?"

"Ah, let's have a lookie-loo," said Maybe as he brought up a series of videos. "As usual, human suffering is number one." They watched a video of a man tripping and falling. "Followed by babies sucking on lemons, cats becoming frightened by zucchinis . . . oh, screaming goats are back, hot-pepper challenges, video-game walk-throughs, unboxings, makeup tutorials, cooking demos, and—lastly—bee puns."

They watched a video of an animated bee buzzing around a daisy. "Let's *bee* friends," it said. The flower winked at it

"Ugh," Ralph and Vanellope said in unison.

"All right, you don't have to do any bee puns," Yesss said.

"Oh, I'm doing a bee pun," Ralph retorted. "And I'm eating a hot pepper and I'm putting on makeup. I'm doing all those things." He was determined to earn hearts and make the money they needed.

"This is what the Internet was invented for," Yesss said excitedly. "I love you."

"Kid! We're totally gonna save your game!" Ralph exclaimed.

"And I know just how to start!" said Yesss. The three quickly got to work.

👍

Later that day, in an office cubicle, a laid-back employee named Lee scrolled through BuzzzTube at his computer, looking bored. "Seen it. Saw that one. Seen it. Huh?" He noticed one of Ralph's videos, clicked on it, and watched it play. He let out a small, goofy laugh and turned to one of his office mates. "Yo, McNeely, remember Wreck-It Ralph?"

"That bad guy from the old video game?" asked McNeely.

"Yeah, exactly. I'm gonna send you a super-random video. Check it out, dude." He clicked on a heart, giving the video some love, and sent it off.

Inside BuzzzTube, Lee's avatar appeared, tossing a heart at Ralph's video. McNeely's avatar threw a heart as well.

In one video, Ralph ate a hot pepper that was so spicy, it sent him banging around the kitchen. In another, he presented a cooking tutorial, during

which he burned a pie and his hair caught on fire!
With each ridiculous video that users watched, they
continued to give Ralph hearts. It seemed the plan
just might work! But the truth was . . . they were
running out of time.

Yesss had one more idea.

Chapter 12

Yesss paced as she addressed an army of pop-ups like a drill sergeant. "This man is on fire. Literal and figurative fire," she said. "But this genius still needs two hundred million hearts in the next five hours or this child loses her game." Yesss pointed to Vanellope, who nodded solemnly. "That's why I'm on to phase two: you, my elite pop-up army. I need you out there popping up and getting clicks at all the social media and entertainment websites. I'm talking Tumblr, Instagram, Mashable. . . . This isn't just a marketing campaign! This is an all-out viral assault! Let's get this man his hearts!"

The pop-ups marched out of the hangar as Vanellope stepped up to Yesss. "That looks like fun. Hey, Yesss—I wanna go, too."

"Hmmm, I don't know," said Yesss. "Can you be annoyingly aggressive?"

Vanellope began poking her nonstop. "I don't know. Can I? Can I? Can I?"

"Yeah, you're perfect." Yesss handed her a pop-up sign. "Here."

"Hey, I wanna go!" Ralph said.

"No, baby. You have to stay here and make the videos," Yesss told him.

"Yeah, Ralph," Vanellope said. "That's kinda the whole point."

"Okay, but . . . ," said Ralph. "I just don't know if it's a good idea for you to go out on the Internet by yourself."

"What exactly is the issue here? You think I can't take care of myself?" she said.

"No, but if we're being honest, I sometimes have to question your judgment," said Ralph. "You tend to have bad taste in friends."

Vanellope paused, confused. "What? YOU are my best friend."

Ralph nodded. "Case in point."

Vanellope looked at him. "Ralph, come on. It's my game we're trying to save. I wanna help."

Ralph didn't like the idea at all. "But the Internet is really big. What if you get lost?"

"She won't," said Yesss. "She'll be in my personal web-browsing limo, which has GPS. And your app comes with BuzzzFace, so you can keep in touch anywhere on the Internet." With that, she ushered Vanellope toward her limo.

"I don't know," Ralph said, still hesitant about the plan.

"Ralph, I'll be fine," reassured Vanellope.

"But we've never really been apart in six years."

"*You'll* be fine," said Vanellope. "It's just a few measly hours. Focus on what's important: getting that wheel."

Her words brought Ralph back to reality. "Yeah, you're right."

Vanellope hopped into the limo. "You and me, we'll be celebrating this time tomorrow," she said to Ralph as the doors closed. Then she turned to Maybe. "All right, Jeeves! Take me to where the action is."

The limo blasted off, leaving Ralph and Yesss behind. Ralph turned to Yesss. "Where are you sending her?"

She pulled up a holographic globe of the Internet that glowed brightly. "Since candy girl comes from an arcade game, I'm thinking she'd be good in the gaming district."

Ralph's eyes widened as he saw the *Slaughter Race* icon appear on the map. That was the *last* place he wanted her to go. "Actually, why don't you send her somewhere a little more . . ." Ralph spun the globe, searching for the best and safest site for Vanellope. "How 'bout fan sites? She is technically a princess, so maybe you could send her to this one with the castle."

"Good call," said Yesss. "I'm redirecting our newest little pop-up to the happiest place online."

A little later, Vanellope gazed around the busy site called OhMyDisney.com. "Wow, this place is bonkers!" she said. Avatars flitted around characters of all shapes and sizes, clicking on everything around them. "Sheesh, is there anything this Disney joint *doesn't* own?" she said to herself.

"If there is, they'll buy it eventually," answered Eeyore in his deep monotone. The gray donkey looked at Vanellope with his sad eyes and then slowly moved on.

Vanellope turned around to see a quiz taking place nearby.

An announcer said, "Your last question—'My friends would describe me as . . .'"

In the real world, a girl read the options: "'Smart, funny, kind, brave.'" She thought it over before clicking on her answer. "Um, I guess kind."

"Based on your answers," said the announcer, "your princess BFF is . . . Snow White!"

Everyone applauded as Snow White stepped forward and took her place in the spotlight.

"I do believe our friendship shall be the fairest of them all!" Snow White said sweetly.

Vanellope followed an avatar looking to click on something and said, "Wanna meet *my* BFF? It's Wreck-It Ralph. Click here to see his newest video."

"Is Wreck-It Ralph a Disney character?" asked the princess avatar.

"Sure," said Vanellope. "Why not."

The avatar clicked on Vanellope's pop-up and was immediately whisked away in a pod to BuzzzTube.

Vanellope headed over to another crowd and

managed to get more avatars to click. "It's almost too easy," she said to herself. But as she spun around to find more avatars, a security guard stopped her.

"Hey, do you have a permit for that pop-up?" asked the guard.

"Urm . . ."

"That's unauthorized clickbait," said another guard. "You're coming with us."

"Uh, click here," said Vanellope. Just as the guard grabbed for her, she hit him with her sign and he zoomed off to BuzzzTube.

Vanellope turned and bolted as more guards appeared, joining in the chase. She ran through the site, desperately looking for an escape route, until she found herself trapped in a corridor.

Vanellope looked left and right, but there was nowhere to run.

Chapter 13

With the guards right behind her, Vanellope pushed against the only door in sight—a locked one labeled PRINCESSES. She struggled for a moment, trying to glitch inside.

By the time the guards arrived, she was gone. "Any sign of her?" one asked.

"No—maybe she went down to the *Air Bud* pavilion," said the other. They set out to continue their search.

On the other side of the locked door was a lovely dressing room where Vanellope came face to face with the Oh My Disney princesses!

"Uh, hi," Vanellope said awkwardly.

The princesses leaped into action, ready to protect

themselves. Mulan held her sword, Rapunzel gripped her frying pan, and Belle clutched a book. Cinderella smashed her glass slipper and waved its jagged edge—just in case.

"Whoa, whoa, ladies! I can explain," said Vanellope, holding up her hands. "See, um, I'm a princess, too."

"Wait, what?" said Anna.

"Yeah, Princess Vanellope von Schweetz of the, uh, *Sugar Rush* von Schweetzes. I'm sure you've heard of us. It'd be kind of embarrassing if you haven't."

"What kind of princess are you?" asked Pocahontas.

"Do you have magic hair?" asked Rapunzel.

"No," answered Vanellope.

"Magic hands?" asked Elsa.

"No."

"Do animals talk to you?" Pocahontas, Jasmine, and Cinderella asked simultaneously.

"No."

"Were you poisoned?" Snow White asked dramatically.

"No."

"Cursed?" asked Aurora and Tiana.

"No."

"Kidnapped or enslaved?" asked Rapunzel, Belle, Cinderella, Elsa, and Anna.

"NO! Are you guys okay? Should I call the police?" asked Vanellope.

"Then I have to assume you made a deal with an underwater sea witch where she took your voice in exchange for a pair of human legs?" said Ariel.

"No! Who would do that?"

"Have you ever had true love's kiss?" asked Snow White.

"Ew! Baaaarf!" said Vanellope, gagging.

"Do you have daddy issues?" asked Jasmine.

"I don't even have a mom," said Vanellope.

Nearly every princess in the room squealed, "Neither do we!"

"And now for the million-dollar question," said Rapunzel. "Do people assume all your problems got solved because a big strong man showed up?"

"YES!" Vanellope shouted without hesitation. "What is *up* with that?"

"She *is* a princess!" they all exclaimed. Snow White trilled with delight.

Cinderella eyed Vanellope's outfit. "Who made your gown?" she asked. "I've never seen anything quite like it."

"Oh, this old thing?" Vanellope said, looking at her casual clothes with a shrug.

"Oh, I'd so love to have one of my own," said Cinderella.

The other princesses agreed, shouting, "As would I!"

"Oh, I want one, too, you guys!" said Ariel.

"I'll get my mice on this," said Cinderella.

A few moments later, all the princesses were enjoying pure comfort as they relaxed in hoodies, sweatpants, and fluffy boots. Each one had their hair tied up in a sloppy knot or ponytail.

"So this is love," said Cinderella. "All hail Princess Vanellope, the queen of comfy!"

The princesses cheered, "Yay, Vanellope!"

"Of all the thingamabobs in this entire world, I never thought I'd get to wear a real . . . what's it called again? Oh, yeah. Shirt." Suddenly, Ariel broke into song: *"I once had a dream that I might wear a shirt—"*

Vanellope's face twisted in confusion. "Whoa, whoa, whoa, what is going on?" she asked.

"She's singing," said Jasmine.

"Yeah, duh. But there was, like, music and a spotlight. You all saw it, right?" asked Vanellope.

"That's what happens when a princess sings about her dreams," explained Tiana.

"I assure you, that has never happened to me. Not once," Vanellope said.

"Well, why don't you try right now?" said Rapunzel. "What is it that you really want? Sing about that."

"Okay, sure. Let's see . . . um . . ." Vanellope cleared her throat and began to sing stiffly, *"Oh, steering wheel. Oh, steering wheel. Yes, I want a steering wheel. . . ."*

The princesses winced as they listened to her out-of-tune attempt.

"Well, there's a lot to unpack there," Belle finally said. "So, this steering wheel you sing of—that's a metaphor?"

"No," Vanellope replied. "No metaphor. I literally

meant a steering wheel. I think the issue is I'm a lousy singer."

"Sometimes your song can't start until you go somewhere to reflect," offered Mulan.

"What works for some of us is finding a body of water and staring at it," Pocahontas said, agreeing with Mulan.

"What?" Vanellope asked.

"Oh, yes!" Snow White exclaimed. "I stare at a wishing well!"

"I stare at the ocean," Moana said.

Mulan raised her hand. "Horse trough," she confessed.

"Soap bubbles!" Cinderella said.

"Wait," said Vanellope. "You're saying if I just stare at some water—"

"*Important* water," Ariel clarified.

"Right, of course," said Vanellope. "Important water. I stare at that and somehow magically I'll start singing about my dream? I don't think so, ladies."

"You'll see," Belle said.

As Vanellope let their words sink in, there was a knock on the dressing-room door. "Five minutes, princesses!" a voice announced. "Another Which Disney Princess Are You? quizlet starts in five minutes."

"I guess it's back to the gowns, girls," said Tiana with a sigh.

"Lovely to meet you, Vanellope," said Aurora.

"Best of luck finding your song," said Belle.

"And may a mouse never leave your girnal with a teardrop in his eye, and may you always be just as happy as wish you to be," Merida said.

"Uh-huh . . . ," Vanellope said. Then she leaned over and asked the others, "What did she just say?"

"We don't know," Moana replied.

"We can't understand her," said Tiana.

"She's from the other studio," Anna added.

Vanellope politely smiled and left the princesses. Her mind was heavy as she departed. She couldn't stop thinking about the song. Could her new friends somehow be right?

Chapter 14

Meanwhile, Ralph and Yesss were busy working on creating a whole new video.

"Hey, guys. Wreck-It Ralph here with a little box I'm gonna open. Let's see," Ralph said as he inspected the box. "Got a little heft to it. Something wobbling around inside. Let's open it up, and—"

But before Ralph could finish his sentence, a swarm of buzzing bees flew out of the box and he screeched!

"Open sesa-*bees*!" said a voice.

Ralph and Yesss edited the video in her office.

"All right," said Yesss, looking at her computer. "Uploading. Who knew a bee pun would be the thing to put us over the top? Genius."

Then the eBoy appeared in front of Ralph. "Hey, mister!" he said cheerfully.

"Oh, hi, eBoy," said Ralph.

"Just here to let you know your bid expires in thirty minutes."

Ralph thanked him, and the eBoy disappeared.

"You hear that, Yesss? We don't have much time," said Ralph.

"Oh, no, oh, no, no, no, no, no, no," said Yesss, her eyes fixed on her computer screen. A bright rainbow-colored wheel appeared, spinning and spinning. "OH, *NO!*" she shouted, frustrated.

"Why are you angry at that lollipop?" asked Ralph. "What's going on?"

"The file's not loading," Yesss answered. "If this thing doesn't load, we're not gonna make it. You don't have enough hearts."

Ralph immediately started to run for the door.

Yesss called out, "Where are you going?"

"I'm going down to the floor to get some hearts!" he shouted as he left the office.

"That's a genius idea," Yesss said. She turned back to her computer, and when the file still hadn't

Ralph thinks his life couldn't be more **perfect**. He has his **best friend**, Vanellope—who he hangs out with every night—and his own **You're My Hero** medal, which she gave him. What else could he want? *Not* the Internet, that's for sure!

VANELLOPE

Vanellope used her ability to **glitch** to become the best racer in *Sugar Rush*. But as much as she loves her game and spending time with Ralph, she can't help **wondering** if there's **something else** out there for her.

The Internet is a busy place with endless websites. Luckily, there's KnowsMore! He runs a **search bar** to help users find exactly what they're looking for in only seconds. Just watch how fast his **autofill** works!

SPAMLEY

Spamley **pops up** when you least expect it. While he's used to being ignored, Ralph and Vanellope take note of his sign, which advertises ways to **get rich** by playing video games.

"MY SISTER-IN-LAW GOT RICH$$ PLAYING GAMES!!!"

THE UNITED

GORD

Gord might not be a netizen of many words, but he's Spamley's **loyal sidekick**. He's always there to lend a **helping arm** or two.

SHANK

Shank is the **coolest**, toughest leader of a racing crew in the very popular Internet game *Slaughter Race*. Vanellope is in **awe** of Shank's driving skills.

Yesss runs the hip, **trendy** BuzzzTube website. She knows how to turn videos into viral sensations—and how to get them as many **hearts** as possible!

FELIX & CALHOUN

While Ralph and Vanellope explore the Internet, Felix and Calhoun realize they will need more than **his hammer** and **her armor** when a group of *Sugar Rush* kids come to live with them!

uploaded, she screamed, "Someone get me tech support!"

Ralph wandered around the main floor of BuzzzTube and found himself staring at a video monitor that was showing a popular meme of a large, fluffy cat stuck inside a small pickle jar. Tons of users were watching it, so Ralph decided to replace it with his own video, forcing the users to watch that instead.

"Here you go! Right here," he shouted. "This is the one you wanna watch." Then he grabbed a hose from a netizen and started sucking up all the hearts he could.

As he was collecting hearts, Ralph noticed a group of avatars walking by. He wanted to get their attention to direct them to his video, so he chased them through a door labeled COMMENTS.

"Anybody in here?" he said. "Hey, come out here and give me some hearts!" But the room was completely empty.

As Ralph looked around, he wondered if he had stumbled into a library of some sort. He spotted his name on a wall and went over to look at it, only to realize the wall was full of comments from various users.

He began reading aloud: "'Wreck-It Ralph is back.'" He laughed and said, "Oh, they're talking about *me*."

Ralph kept reading. "'Wreck-It Ralph? Seriously?'" He was confused, and said to himself, "Darn tootin', I'm serious."

He looked at another: "'*Fix-It Felix Jr.* was my favorite game.'" Ralph smiled and said, "Mine too."

Then he moved on to a different comment. "'Ralph's videos stink.'" His smile faded as he stared at those three words. Yet another user commented with "'So stupid.'" He continued to read one bad comment after another, even the one that had his name misspelled—"'Ralf is THE WORST'"—and, finally, "'I HATE HIM.'"

Ralph couldn't believe it. The people giving him hearts weren't laughing *with* him at all. They were laughing *at* him. Every single comment was cruel.

Yesss entered, looking for Ralph. It broke him out of his spell. "Yo, Ralph! You in here, dude? I gotta show you—"

Ralph turned around and Yesss instantly saw the sadness in his eyes.

"Oh, Ralph. First rule of the Internet: Do not read the comments," she said softly. "Look, this place can bring out the worst in some people. But you gotta ignore all this. This isn't about you. It's about them."

"It's fine," said Ralph. "People always hated me for being a Bad Guy. I didn't have a single friend for the first twenty-seven years of my life. So all this—all these 'hearts' I've been getting? Good reminder that this is the only heart that matters." He pulled out his medal. "As long as Vanellope likes me, I don't need anybody else. And I sure as heck don't need the Internet."

"Okay, well, hold on, now," said Yesss. "It's not all bad. The Internet can also be a place where you find a steering wheel at one website and make enough money to buy it at another one. Congratulations, Ralph," she said, grinning. "You did it."

"Wait, really?" said Ralph, brightening.

Yesss told him to check his account, and he pulled out his Buzzzy device. "You needed twenty-seven thousand and one," she said. "You got over thirty grand."

"All right!" cheered Ralph. "Oh my gosh, this is great! Thank you, Yesss. I couldn't have done it without you."

"That's really true," she said.

"Hey, eBoy!" Ralph called out. "Can you give me a ride?!"

The eBoy appeared and said happily, "You got it, ace!"

On the way, Ralph couldn't wait to tell Vanellope the good news. He reached for his Buzzzy device.

Vanellope sat on an Internet street corner, staring at a puddle intensely, trying to figure out what she really wanted. "C'mon, song," she said to herself. "C'mon, c'mon. What is your dream?" But nothing came to her. "Well, ladies. I tried. No song for this princess."

Suddenly, her Buzzzy device rang, interrupting her thoughts. Vanellope opened her phone, and Ralph's face appeared as a hologram.

"We did it, kid! We got the money!" he said.

"No way. Ralph, that's great," Vanellope said with mixed feelings.

"I'm on my way to eBay with the eBoy now. Meet me out front in five minutes?"

"Okay, I'll see you soon," said Vanellope.

"We're going home, kid! Our lives can finally go back to normal! Woo-hoo!" Ralph said, and hung up.

"Wow. I can't believe it. I get to go . . . home?" Vanellope said quietly. "I guess I do just want a steering wheel." Her excitement suddenly faded as the reality of going back to *Sugar Rush* set in. She knew she was supposed to feel happy, but for some reason, she didn't. After all they had been through, why wasn't she thrilled to know she would be going back home? Vanellope looked at the puddle again and noticed something strange in its reflection. . . .

Chapter 15

In the reflection of the puddle, Vanellope could see . . . *Slaughter Race*! She gasped—and was suddenly transported into the game!

Then something even stranger happened. She began to sing! The song poured out of her, rhymes and all, as she strolled through the high-octane racing game, exploring and admiring its every crazy corner.

The dirty pigeons, smelly rats, fallen wires, and burning tires Vanellope saw all made perfect sense to her. Shank and her crew—even the hungry shark, the appliance thieves, and a creepy clown—joined in and sang along. Odd as it was, they all seemed to coordinate their actions in a ballad that Vanellope somehow loved with all her heart.

Through her song, Vanellope came to realize what she really wanted. Her princess friends had been right! Her heart's true desire was *not* to get the steering wheel and go back home to *Sugar Rush*. It was to stay in *Slaughter Race* and make it her new home! She sang and danced through the game, overjoyed at the revelation, until . . .

The full moon shining above reminded her of Ralph's big head, and her jubilance turned to worry. If she followed her dream, she'd have to leave her best friend behind. Vanellope sat down and sighed. She knew Ralph would be absolutely crushed if he found out she wanted to stay in *Slaughter Race*. But now that she knew her heart's true desire, how could she ignore it?

Ralph, meanwhile, was still focused on his goal. After the eBoy dropped Ralph off at eBay, he slapped his BuzzzyBuxxx card on Elaine's checkout counter. "You'll find more than enough dollars in my account now," he said proudly. "So let's get this show on the road."

"Nothing would make me happier," Elaine said

dryly. "Your *Sugar Rush* steering wheel will ship to Litwak's Family Fun Center today. Congratulations."

"Woo-hoo, yes! That's how you do it, eBoy!" Ralph high-fived him on his way out the door.

"Way to go, champ!" the eBoy said. "That's what I call cookin' with gas."

Ralph waited outside for Vanellope and noticed Spamley nearby, trying to get new customers. When he spotted Ralph, he smiled and said hello.

"What's the good word, brother?" asked Spamley.

Ralph told him that he and Vanellope had made enough money to return home. Spamley was happy, but Ralph barely noticed. He was distracted, wondering where Vanellope was. He asked Spamley if he had seen her.

"Your little chum? No, sir, I have not," replied Spamley.

Ralph pulled out his phone and dialed Vanellope on his BuzzzFace app.

Vanellope and Shank were sitting on the hood of Shank's car in *Slaughter Race*. Vanellope's Buzzzy device began vibrating on the dashboard inside the car, and with each buzz, it crept closer and closer to the edge, until it finally fell onto the floor. As the device hit the seat, the call was answered without Vanellope knowing. Ralph's holographic image appeared behind her.

"See over there—over that mountain?" said Shank, pointing. "That's the Sequoia Speedway. It's gonna be unlocked next month. My favorite coming up is Kawaii Rivals. It's adorable and tough. Kinda like you."

Ralph was shocked to see Vanellope sitting with Shank. "What are you doing in that awful game with her?" he said. But because the device was muted, Vanellope didn't hear him. She continued to chat with Shank.

"The race will end right over there," Shank said. "It's gonna be so tight."

"Wow. I love it," said Vanellope.

Ralph realized they didn't notice his hologram and paused to eavesdrop.

"Hey, can I tell you something that I don't think I could ever tell Ralph?" asked Vanellope.

"Of course. What is it?" said Shank.

"I know it sounds crazy . . . but the second I

walked into this game, it felt, well, it felt like home. I mean, more than *Sugar Rush* ever did."

"Oh, yeah? How so?" asked Shank.

"Cause it's like my dream world," Vanellope admitted. "It's full of weirdos, and the racing is super dangerous, and you never know what's going to happen next. I mean, back home I know exactly what's gonna happen next, cause Ralph's dream is to do the same thing every day."

"There's no law saying best friends have to have the same dreams," Shank said.

"Whoa, yeah," said Vanellope, taking in her words. "You are a very wise person, Shank. And a good friend, too. Thank you."

"You can just say 'Shank you' if you want," she said with a smirk.

Vanellope laughed and gazed out at *Slaughter Race*.

"You know," said Shank, "you can always come visit any time you want after you get your life back to normal."

"I don't want my life to be normal," Vanellope said. "I want *this* to be my life. I want to stay here. I can't go home. I just can't."

Unable to bear hearing another word, Ralph ended the call. He felt like someone had punched him in the heart.

"Well, that right there is a kick in the teeth, friend," said Spamley, who had been watching the whole thing over Ralph's shoulder.

"I can't believe it," said Ralph. "I thought she was supposed to be my best friend."

"A straight-up donkey kick," Spamley added, shaking his head.

"She's been brainwashed," said Ralph. "That's what this is. Cause the Vanellope I know would never abandon me. I gotta get her outta there right away."

"Easy, now, tiger," said Spamley. "I admire the impulse, but you charge in there like some kinda white knight, she's liable to hold it against you."

"So, what—I'm supposed to let her stay in a game that's obviously bad for her?" said Ralph.

"Course not," said Spamley.

"Then how do I make her leave, huh? She thinks it's so great and exciting in there. I mean, unless there's a way to slow down the game and make it boring, I dunno what to do," said Ralph.

Spamley tapped a finger against his nose and checked to make sure no one was watching. With the coast clear, he whispered, "There's ways." He gestured to Ralph to follow and said, "Come with me."

Chapter 16

Ralph followed Spamley down a dark alley where creepy characters spoke in hushed voices to each other in the shadows. Ralph overheard one say "I got mother's maiden names, social security numbers . . ." before he returned his attention to his companion.

"Now, this area down here is what's called the Dark Net," explained Spamley. "Lotta shady characters hang out down here, so try to keep a low profile. GORD!" At Spamley's call, Gord instantly appeared beside them. "Oh, there you are," said Spamley. He turned to Ralph. "Now, Gord here, he has dabbled in virus making. But his cousin, the guy we're going to see—big ol' son of a gun who goes by the name of Double Dan—this dude is a virus-making machine." Spamley stopped at a door with cracked paint around its edges. "Here we go." He slowly turned the knob.

Ralph paused and whispered, "Are you sure this is safe?"

"Oh, of course it is. Just whatever you do—do *not* look at his little brother," warned Spamley.

"His little brother?" asked Ralph, confused.

The door creaked as Spamley pushed it open and entered. Ralph and Gord followed him into the rundown site.

A huge worm, Double Dan, worked at a lab table, stirring strange-looking liquids inside glass beakers.

"Double Dan!" said Spamley. "Long time no see. How ya doing, chum?"

Double Dan looked up, annoyed. "Who are you?"

"JP Spamley. We met one time over at Friendster, which tells you it's been a little bit. . . ."

Even though he tried to avoid it, Spamley's eyes drifted toward Double Dan's neck, where a small, squishy face stuck out and uttered a squeak. It was none other than his brother, Little Dan. Double Dan reached out and grabbed Spamley by the throat. "What are you looking at?"

"Nothing," Spamley said quickly.

"You looking at my brother?" Double Dan asked in a threatening tone.

"No, sir," answered Spamley.

"I saw you," said Double Dan.

"Never."

"Don't you look at my little brother," ordered Double Dan.

"I wasn't," said Spamley, working extra hard to keep his eyes away from Double Dan's neck.

"He's very self-conscious." Double Dan hurled Spamley at the wall and turned to Ralph. "Now," he said, taking a step closer. "What are *you* doing here?"

Ralph tried his best not to stare at Little Dan, but when Double Dan started to make an odd noise, Ralph couldn't help looking. "The reason I came to your neck of the face . . . ," Ralph began, stumbling over his words. "I mean, there's a face in your neck. I mean woods. Neck of the woods . . .

The reason I'm here is because I heard a tumor—a *rumor*—that you could give me a harmless virus to slow down the *Slaughter Race* game?"

"Mmm, yes," said Double Dan. "My cousin Gordon told me that you want to crash it." Gord popped out from behind Spamley and waved hello to Double Dan.

"Crash it?" said Ralph. "No, no, no. I don't want anyone getting hurt." He watched nervously as Double Dan grunted and went to work, searching through various drawers and removing a variety of chemicals. "If there's a way to just, I dunno, make the cars go slow or something, just so the game is boring and my friend comes back home to me. That's all."

Double Dan bent down and picked up a wooden container.

"Allow me to introduce you to Arthur," he said. He opened the box and revealed a terrifying virus that made both Ralph and Spamley shriek. "Arthur's what I call an insecurity virus. Means he looks for little flaws and glitches that make a program insecure. You release him into that *Slaughter Race* game, and Arthur will find some defect in the code. Then what he'll do is he'll make millions of copies of said defect and he'll distribute the copies all over the game. And that is guaranteed to slow everything down in there and make the game quote/unquote 'boring,' just like you want." Double Dan placed the virus back in the box and closed it before handing it to Ralph.

"Okay, and just to be super clear here . . . no one gets hurt, right?" asked Ralph.

"Are you stupid?" asked Double Dan.

"Um—I . . . ," Ralph stuttered.

"Because the only way anyone gets hurt is if you are stupid. All you have to do is make sure the virus stays in *Slaughter Race.*"

"Don't be stupid and let the virus out of *Slaughter Race,*" repeated Ralph. "Goiter it. Er—*got it,* got it."

"GET OUT!" shouted Double Dan.

"Thank you, you're a cyst face," Ralph said, inching toward the door. "I mean, *assistance.* Thank you for you're a cyst face. Assistance. You know what I mean. Goodbye!" He clutched the box and hurried out, more ready than ever to get his best friend back for good.

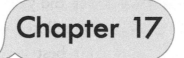

Chapter 17

Vanellope was having a wonderful time playing basketball with the crew in *Slaughter Race*. She impressed everyone by sinking a behind-the-back free throw to win the game.

"Oh, fiddlesticks. That's game," groaned Pyro.

"Beginner's luck," said Vanellope with a shrug.

"Aw, come on, kid. I know a hustle when I see one," said Debbie, laughing.

A courier zipped by on a moped and announced that a player was on the way. Everyone headed toward their cars, gearing up for the race.

"Showtime," said Shank, walking alongside Vanellope. "You ready for your first race?"

"I think so," said Vanellope. But then she began to glitch.

Shank told Vanellope not to be nervous. She tried to encourage her, but Vanellope continued glitching.

"You didn't tell Ralph yet, did you?" asked Shank.

"Not exactly," replied Vanellope.

"Come on, V. He's your best friend. You gotta let him know you're planning on staying here for a while."

"He's gonna get so upset," said Vanellope.

Shank stopped and turned to Vanellope. "Yeah, he might. But you guys will work it out."

"What if we don't?" asked Vanellope. "What if his feelings get hurt so bad that he doesn't want to be my friend anymore?"

"Look, all friendships change," Shank told her. "And the good ones—they get stronger because of it."

A horn honked and Butcher Boy yelled to them from his car, "I don't wanna bother you, Shank, but the player is waiting."

Shank turned her attention back to Vanellope. "I'm not gonna tell you what to do, kid. It's your call," she said.

"Okay . . . ," replied Vanellope, still unsure what

to do. But she had no time to think—the race was about to begin.

"Let's race!" said Shank, jumping into her car and peeling out.

While Vanellope was busy climbing into her own car, Ralph had managed to release the virus into *Slaughter Race*. Immediately, it began scanning the area for insecurities.

The race started and a player quickly caught up to Shank, managing to force her into a wall. Shank struggled as she tried to break free, spinning her wheels. Vanellope appeared and mimicked the move she had seen Shank do when they met. She sped up a ramp and launched herself into the air, landing directly in front of the startled player. He crashed, and Shank escaped!

"Power drift into a drift jump!" Shank said, cheering. "You're amazing!"

Vanellope giggled. "Thank you!"

Meanwhile, the worm continued searching every inch of the game for insecurities, climbing up buildings and scanning different players' cars.

"Looks like we're not finished. C'mon, V. Let's

take this guy!" said Shank as the player regenerated from his crash in the near distance.

But Vanellope was distracted. Something had caught her eye on top of a building. It resembled Ralph. Vanellope spun out and slowed to a stop to take another look. She realized it wasn't Ralph, but an inflatable gorilla! The thought of Ralph made Vanellope glitch, and she began to panic. "Okay. Relax. Relax," she said, trying to calm herself. "Just call him after the race. It'll be okay."

The worm squirming nearby detected Vanellope's glitch and recognized it as an insecurity. It quickly copied the glitch and distributed it throughout the entire game! Suddenly, some of the buildings around her began to flash. She looked around, confused and shocked to see more and more parts of the game breaking down . . . and then everything was glitching! Not knowing what else to do, she raced off to find Shank.

Watching from outside the game, Ralph and Spamley could see that things weren't right.

"What's going on, Spamley?" asked Ralph. "The whole website's going crazy. I thought that virus was only supposed to slow down the game."

"It was!" sputtered Spamley. "It must have found something real unstable in there."

Ralph knew right away. "It's her glitch," he said. "Oh, man. I gotta get her out of there. Spamley, you better go tell Double Dan."

"You got it," said Spamley. As Ralph bolted toward the entrance of *Slaughter Race,* Spamley shouted back to him, "Remember not to let the virus get outta that game!"

"Come on, kid!" yelled Shank. "The game is crashing! We gotta get you out of here."

"I think it's my glitch," said Vanellope. "I don't know how this is happening!"

"It doesn't matter. We'll be fine! But we have to get you out of here before the game reboots! Follow me to the exit!" urged Shank.

Vanellope and the other racers followed Shank out as the game began to fall apart. Clouds of dust filled the air as buildings crumbled to the ground and smashed to bits. A towering skyscraper fell down, separating Vanellope from the group. She tried to swerve out of the way, but a beam fell on her car, trapping her.

Ralph searched through the rubble. "Kid! Kid! Where are you?" he shouted.

"The server is rebooting, Ralph!" Shank said. "Both of you have to get out of here *now*!"

Finally, Ralph spotted Vanellope and pulled her out of the wreckage. "There you are. Come on, stay with me!" he said. But Vanellope didn't respond. He threw her over his shoulder and bolted out of the game, dodging falling debris along the way.

Outside *Slaughter Race,* the firewalls started to close. Ralph punched a hole in one of the walls and dove through. He and Vanellope spilled onto the ground outside the game.

"C'mon, Vanellope, wake up," Ralph begged desperately. "Come on. I can't live without you."

Vanellope's eyes fluttered open. "Ralph," she said weakly.

"Oh, thank goodness," he said, relieved.

"I messed up so bad, Ralph," said Vanellope sadly.

"No, kid," said Ralph. "It's not your fault."

"Yes, it is!" Vanellope shouted. "This is all because of me and my glitch. What was I thinking? You were right." She looked at Ralph. "This was a dumb idea, a stupid dream. . . ."

She started to cry, and Ralph put his arms around her. "Hey, it's okay," he said. Ralph searched his mind, trying to find the right words to cheer her up. "There's . . . there's no law saying friends have to have the same dreams," he added.

Vanellope stopped sobbing and looked up at him. "What did you say?" she asked.

"What did I say?" said Ralph.

She pulled away from him, sniffling. "'There's no law saying friends have to have the same dreams'— where did you hear that?" she asked.

"Um, where did I hear that?" Ralph fumbled, wishing he had kept his mouth shut.

"Hey, how did you know to rescue me in *Slaughter Race*?" asked Vanellope, now suspicious that there was something Ralph wasn't telling her.

Ralph sighed. He knew he was busted. "Look, the attachment was just supposed to slow down the game. . . ."

"Attachment?" Vanellope asked, confused.

Ralph explained that the virus he let loose was

supposed to be harmless, but Vanellope couldn't believe what she was hearing.

"*You* did this?" asked Vanellope, her voice rising in anger.

"Well, I wouldn't have done anything if I hadn't heard you tell Shank that you wanted to live in *Slaughter Race* forever," Ralph said defensively.

"Ah, so you *spied* on me," said Vanellope. "This just gets better by the minute."

"Hey, you're not exactly innocent here. You were gonna ditch everybody and abandon *Sugar Rush*," said Ralph.

"Come on, I'm one of eleven racers. They'd never miss me."

"Well, what about me?" asked Ralph.

"You?" said Vanellope, now fuming. "Why would I ever spend another second with you after what you did?" She grabbed Ralph's medal and threw it.

"No!" Ralph gasped as the medal fell to the ground. He looked to see Vanellope running away.

"I'm going back to find Shank. Don't even think about following me!" she said, disappearing.

Ralph had never felt so low. Even though Vanellope was gone, he spoke out loud as if she were there. "Vanellope, what am I supposed to do? What do I do?"

While he sat alone, the virus worm squirmed through the firewall hole and exited *Slaughter Race*. It quickly picked up on Ralph, finding him to be one hundred percent insecure. Without anyone noticing, it copied Ralph's insecurity . . . and began to distribute it all over the Internet.

Ralph made his way down to the Older Net—the part of the Internet where spam mail and expired websites were discarded—to retrieve his medal. When he finally found it, he discovered it had split in two. He sighed and sat on a mound of garbage. "You are such an idiot," he said.

Just then, he noticed something coming toward him. Something that looked an awful lot like . . . himself.

Chapter 18

As Vanellope walked away from Ralph, she headed toward the Internet's hub, where she and Ralph first arrived. She was on a mission to get as far away from him as possible when suddenly, she saw Ralph coming around the corner. She couldn't believe her eyes.

"What is your problem, Ralph? I told you not to follow me!" Vanellope shouted.

But something was off. He didn't say anything. Instead, he started to run toward her. Vanellope screamed and ran away!

Vanellope quickly realized it wasn't Ralph chasing her at all. It was a clone! Soon a horde of similar clones started to follow.

Vanellope stopped and turned around to see that she was in far more trouble than she'd thought. She looked up and saw an astonishing sight. She wasn't being chased by just one Ralph clone—but millions! The army of Ralph clones was taking over the Internet, climbing every website, and destroying everything in its path!

"Sweet mother of Ralph," said Vanellope as the clones wreaked havoc.

An announcement played on a website. "In breaking news," the news anchor said, "the Internet is under assault as a massive service attack crashes websites and clogs servers across the web. The so-called 'Wreck-It Ralph' virus is fast-moving and destructive. Experts are still trying to understand who or what the virus's intended target may be."

Vanellope didn't have time to think. As the news ended, several of the clones spotted her and she was back to running away as fast as she could.

At his Search Bar, KnowsMore was helping answer a user's question. "I found one hundred and thirty results for 'Where does my high school girlfriend live now?'" he said.

"Mr. KnowsMore!" Vanellope shouted as she reached him.

He was absolutely thrilled to see Vanellope. He'd been so busy answering questions for users that he had no clue what was happening around him. "Oh, delightful! You're that courteous little cherub who says 'please' and 'thank you.' What can KnowsMore help you find today?"

Vanellope tried to tell him what was wrong, but she was out of breath. "There's . . . a . . . whole . . ."

"A Whole Foods, a hole in the ozone, *Whole Lotta Love* by British rockers Led Zeppelin," said KnowsMore. His autofill was still rapidly trying to guess her question.

"A whole bunch of Ralphs chasing me!" she blurted.

KnowsMore looked behind Vanellope and saw the clones making their way toward them. "Well, isn't that interesting?" he said. "This would probably be an appropriate time to shutter my site."

Vanellope helped KnowsMore close the shutters. They were safe for now, but it wouldn't last long. They could hear the Ralph clones banging against the shutters and doors outside, trying hard to get in. Vanellope and KnowsMore stacked and piled as many books as they could against the door to create a barrier.

"How long do you think we can hold them back, KnowsMore?" asked Vanellope.

"For precisely one second," he answered.

Just then, the door blasted open and a Ralph clone lunged for Vanellope. She reached for a lamp and used it to hit him over the head.

"Ow! It's me! It's me!" the clone shouted.

But Vanellope hadn't heard the clones actually speak before. "Ralph?"

"I'm so glad you're okay. I followed those things here. I think they're looking for you, kid," he said. It was the real Ralph after all!

Vanellope was relieved, but still furious. "Yeah, ya think?" she shot back.

More loud noises erupted as the clones tried to break through the barricades. They weren't slowing down. Ralph and Vanellope needed a plan—and fast!

"What did you do?" Vanellope asked Ralph.

"I don't know," he replied. "I'm so sorry. I don't know how this happened."

Luckily, they were with someone who did. "It happened because an insecurity virus cloned all of your needy, clingy, self-destructive behavior," KnowsMore said. "The very behavior which, left unchecked, can destroy friendships and, in this particular case, may also destroy the entire Internet. Isn't that interesting?"

"So wrecking *Slaughter Race* wasn't enough for you, huh?" Vanellope asked Ralph.

"I didn't mean to do it. I know I screwed up bad. I know I did," Ralph started to say. But at this point, he wasn't sure what would make Vanellope forgive him. Desperate, he turned to KnowsMore. "You got all the answers. Whadda we do here? How do we get rid of these things?"

The question triggered KnowsMore's search mode and he immediately came back with an answer. "I found two results for your query. Either you put all of the clones in therapy, or," he said as he grabbed a book from his shelves, "alternatively, there's an archway in the Anti-Virus District made out of security software. If Vanellope could some-how lead the clones through that arch, the security software would delete them all at once. It's sort of a codependent Pied Piper situation."

"Wait," Vanellope said. "We know a Pied Piper."

"We do?" Ralph asked.

"Yesss," Vanellope said.

"Who is it?"

"Yesss!"

"Yes what? Oh," Ralph said, finally getting it. "You mean Yesss!"

"Yes!" Vanellope exclaimed.

Just then, a limo flew in and pulled up beside Ralph and Vanellope. It was Yesss! Ralph and Vanellope hopped into the limo and escaped with her.

"Thanks for your help, KnowsMore!" Ralph shouted back to their friend.

KnowsMore looked around his site and saw how badly damaged it was. "Bit of an empty gesture at this point, wouldn't you say?" he said.

But the Ralph clones weren't done yet. Until they had Vanellope, they were willing to demolish everything in their path.

Chapter 19

Moments later, Ralph and Vanellope sat in Yesss's limo. Vanellope sat next to Yesss, still fuming over Ralph.

"I can't believe he did this," she said to Yesss.

"I've seen it a lot, actually," said Yesss. "Not to this extent, of course. But I'm telling you, reading the comments, listening to the hate those trolls spew—it can make a person do some crazy, horrible things."

"Whaddaya mean? What comments?"

"Oh, he didn't tell you? Ralph got trolled hard for those videos he made for you. Bunch of anonymous bullies calling him fat and ugly and useless, saying 'I hate you.'"

"Oh, no," Vanellope said, feeling bad.

"Yeah, and I thought he was handling it. Cause he said as long as he had you, he was okay," said Yesss.

But Vanellope wasn't listening to Yesss anymore. She hung her head, ashamed of the way she had treated Ralph and conflicted about her feelings.

Yesss continued. "I mean, dude obviously made some real bad choices here. But he also made a bee pun video to help his best friend, so . . . life's complicated, isn't it?"

Vanellope nodded. Yesss was right. Life really was complicated, and in that moment, she had an idea that could possibly save all of them—and the Internet.

The limo flew close to the clones and Vanellope called to them, "Yoo-hoo! Up here! It's me, your bestest friend in the whole wide world, who you can't live without!"

One of the clones instantly stopped wrecking things and began chasing her. Soon a hundred more clones appeared, following behind. Vanellope couldn't believe it! She turned back to see thousands of clones following the limo, trying to get to her. The plan was working!

"Wow," said Ralph. "From this view, I can see how I do look pretty needy and clingy and self-destructive. I don't blame you for not wanting to be my friend anymore."

"I never said I don't want to be your friend. I said you were *acting* like a bad friend, which you were," said Vanellope. "But no matter where I live or what I do, I will always be your friend, Ralph. And that will never change."

"How do you know that?" he asked.

"I don't know. I just do," she said.

"Hey, guys," Yesss said, breaking in. "That's the Anti-Virus District straight ahead. We're gonna make it!"

The limo made its way to the Anti-Virus arch even though the Ralph clones were hot on their trail.

"We're gonna make it!" cheered Ralph.

But as they celebrated, the millions of clones clustered together and climbed on top of each other to form a giant, rippling wave. The wave rose, then came down hard, crashing right into the limo, causing it to fly out of control and straight through a Pinterest window!

Ralph, Vanellope, and Yesss crawled out of the car, carefully stepping away from the broken glass. "You guys okay?" asked Ralph.

"I'm fine," said Vanellope, dusting herself off.

"All good. We can still do this," said Yesss. "Come on, big man, help me turn this thing over." Yesss and Ralph worked to lift the limo.

Vanellope noticed a sudden quiet. She looked around curiously, wondering where all the clones had gone. Then she saw them.

"Um, guys?" she said, her jaw nearly hitting the ground. Ralph and Yesss turned to see what Vanellope was gawking at: the millions of clones had gathered again, but this time they formed an enormous and terrifying giant Ralph! The massive clone focused on them, its huge eyes peering over a rooftop.

"That is unsettling," said Ralph. "Get Vanellope outta here now," he added as Giant Ralph began to climb up the side of a tall building. Vanellope was worried about him, but Ralph insisted she go. Then he grabbed a huge one-hundred-foot-long pushpin from a website and stepped toward the beast. "Hey, you! You keep away from her!" he yelled, wielding the pin like a club. "I'm gonna wreck it!" He ran, jumped, and swung with all his might. "She's not your friend. She's *my* friend!" he yelled.

As Ralph battled the beast, Yesss led Vanellope toward an exit. Vanellope paused, looking back at Ralph, but Yesss forced her toward a website, trying to help her escape.

With a flick of its giant finger, the colossal clone hurled Ralph and threw the pin at him. Ralph winced as it blazed by, missing him by a hair. He quickly grabbed the pin and chucked it at Giant Ralph, knocking him off-balance. Giant Ralph staggered into the website that Vanellope and Yesss were running through, causing it to sway. Vanellope was thrown clear off the site, and she clung to the side of a nearby building. She screamed as she began to lose her grip, dangling off the edge.

"Kid! Hang on! Hang on!" Ralph called.

The building trembled and Vanellope fell. Surprisingly, Giant Ralph reached over and caught her in its giant hand!

"Let go of me!" shouted Vanellope. But the beast held her in its clutches and took off running.

"Kid! Kid!" said Ralph, chasing them. "Hey,

hey, get back here! You put her down! Vanellope!" Ralph jumped up onto another website, but the massive Ralph knocked it over. Ralph dove into an email truck just in time and managed to avoid being crushed, but he could only watch helplessly as Giant Ralph, still holding Vanellope, began to scale the towering Google site. At the very top, Giant Ralph paused and looked at Vanellope.

"You know, you're acting like a real Bad Guy here!" she shouted.

The clones grunted angrily. They didn't like hearing her say that.

Meanwhile, Ralph snagged a flying email truck, which he used to get to the top of the website.

"Sheesh, so sensitive," Vanellope said to the clones, not backing down. Suddenly, she came up with an escape plan. "Hey! Wanna play I spy?"

Giant Ralph grunted and nodded.

"That's right," she said. "I spy with my little eye . . . something that's big and yellow and is right behind you!"

Giant Ralph looked around and didn't see anything, which gave Vanellope a chance to run.

Meanwhile, the real Ralph had been scaling the website. He saw Vanellope jump and safely caught her. "I gotcha, kid!" he said.

"What are you doing?" Vanellope asked.

"I'm saving you!" he replied.

"I was handling it, Ralph. I was just about to get away!"

"Well, how was I supposed to know that?"

"Where do you think you're even going?" Vanellope asked.

"I don't know," Ralph answered honestly. "I didn't think that far ahead."

They finally reached the top of the highest construction block they could find. But Giant Ralph caught up—and grabbed Vanellope and Ralph! It held Vanellope in its left hand while it squeezed Ralph in its right hand with all its might.

"Stop it!" shouted Vanellope. "You're squishing him! You're gonna kill him!" Giant Ralph wouldn't stop squeezing. "Take me! You can have me all to yourself! Just put him down. I'll be your only friend."

"No, kid," Ralph pleaded.

"That's it," Vanellope said reassuringly to Giant Ralph. "Put him down and take me. I know that's what you want."

"No! That is not what *I* want!" Ralph said. "It's not right to hold a friend back from her dreams. You don't own her. That's not how friendship works. You need to let her go."

Suddenly, Giant Ralph stopped to listen to what Ralph was saying.

"You need to let her go. I know it's gonna hurt a little bit when you do. Heck, who am I kidding? It's gonna hurt *a lot*. But you're gonna be okay," Ralph said. Then he said to Vanellope, "And we're gonna be okay—right, kid?"

"Of course we are," Vanellope said. "Always."

Giant Ralph blinked as the words settled in. It lowered its huge hand and gently set Vanellope on top of a nearby website.

"Thanks, buddy," Vanellope said.

"I feel good about this," Ralph said.

One by one, the clones began to disappear. "Ralph, look!" said Vanellope. "I think you fixed your insecurity!"

Relieved, Ralph cheered, "Woo-hoo!" But once

they'd all disappeared, he had nothing left to hold on to—and he was a thousand feet above the ground! "Oh, no!" he screamed as he began to fall.

"Ralph! No!" Vanellope shouted.

Just before Ralph crashed into the ground, the Oh My Disney princesses swooped in and rescued him.

"Look! Up there!" Belle exclaimed. "It's a big strong man in need of rescuing!"

All the princesses sprang into action. They worked together to help, each one using her own special skill. Moana made a wave that Elsa froze so Ralph could slide down it before launching into the air again. With a variety of objects, including dresses, a poison apple, and a rope made out of hair, they had built a "hairachute" to slow Ralph's fall.

"The hairachute is working, you guys!" Ariel said.

Pocahontas used her wind power to push Ralph's chute toward a mattress website, causing him to land on top of a plush, comfy bed.

Tiana brought a frog over to kiss him, and when he awoke, he looked around, confused.

"Who are you guys?" he asked.

"Oh, we're with Vanellope," Pocahontas explained.

"Yeah, any friend of Vanellope's is a friend of ours," added Elsa.

Moana looked at Ralph and smiled. "You're welcome."

It wasn't long before journalists reported the good news: "Internet users are breathing a collective sigh of relief. Just as mysteriously as it had appeared, the Wreck-It Ralph virus has now vanished."

Ralph and Vanellope sat on a bench at a bus stop in the Internet.

"Y'know what I just realized?" said Ralph. "The sun never rises or sets here. Cause everything's always on."

"Well, now, isn't that an astute observation," said Vanellope.

"I know," said Ralph with a grin. "Other than KnowsMore, I'm probably the smartest guy in the Internet."

Vanellope agreed and giggled.

Shank called out from the entrance to *Slaughter Race* across the street. "Hey, V. We're about to come back online. You ready?"

"Be right there!" shouted Vanellope.

"Don't be a stranger, Ralph!" said Shank.

"I can't be much stranger than you," replied Ralph.

"Ooh, that's a good dad joke," Shank laughed as she entered *Slaughter Race*.

Vanellope turned to Ralph, trying to figure out what to say next. "Hey, don't forget—Shank added my code and everything, so I'll be able to regenerate. I'll be totally safe."

"No, I know. It's gonna be great. You'll be fine. You found your dream game."

"Yeah, I did. I did. So, I should probably . . . head in there now, you know. . . ."

"Oh, before you go, I wanted to give you this." Ralph reached into his pocket and handed her half of his broken heart medal.

"Oh, gosh. I'm so sorry I broke it," said Vanellope.

"No, no, it's okay. Now we can both have a half. See?" Ralph showed her his half, hanging around his neck.

Vanellope jumped into his arms and hugged him tightly. Their medals came together to form a complete heart.

"I love you so much," she said. "I'm really gonna miss you."

"I'm gonna miss you, too," said Ralph. "All right, okay. Getting a little clingy on me. Get outta here. The world's waiting for ya, kid."

She sprang out of his arms and ran toward *Slaughter Race.* Just before she reached the entrance, she looked back to see Ralph standing there with a hand up, smiling through his tears. A car sped by between them, and when it had passed, Vanellope was gone. Ralph turned and walked away alone.

Chapter 20

A few months later, Ralph sat in Game Central Station at Litwak's Family Fun Center and Arcade, talking on the phone with Vanellope.

"I'll be honest," Ralph said, "it still feels kinda weird around here. I mean, a lot has changed. Even though we got the wheel and saved *Sugar Rush,* it's never really gonna be the same. For starters, the racers aren't even that obnoxious anymore. Raising ten kids has changed Felix and Calhoun, too." He went on to mention that even Surge Protector had noticed and complimented Felix and Calhoun on a job well done.

"I'm also keeping busy," Ralph said, and told her about a book club he'd joined.

"Oh, and we got this new thing we do every

Friday night where we all go hang out in a different game. I actually hosted this week," explained Ralph. He'd set up picnic tables and games out by his brick pile and everyone had a great time. He even brought burned pie—a recipe he'd found on the Internet. "We really do have a lot of fun." Ralph was grateful. "I guess that's pretty much all the news I got for you."

Vanellope smiled, her hologram hovering above Ralph's Buzzzy device as the two chatted. "Well, your stories never disappoint," she said. "I just wish we could hang out sooner."

"When'd you say you were getting those days off?" Ralph asked.

"Like, three months from now," Vanellope said.

"It'll go by in a flash," Ralph said. "Hey, you want me to bring you anything from home when I visit?"

"You know what's impossible to find on the Internet?" said Vanellope. "A halfway decent burger." She missed the ones she and Ralph used to eat together in the arcade.

"I'll bring you guys a truckload," Ralph said. Just then, he noticed some characters heading toward their games as daylight began to break. "Well, the sun's coming up already. Guess I better get to it."

"Yup. Me too," Vanellope said. "Talk next week?"

"I shall await your call," he said.

"Then adieu," Vanellope said to her friend. "Farting is such sweet sorrow. So long, Stink Brain!"

"Bye, kid," Ralph said.

Vanellope's hologram disappeared, and Ralph closed his eyes for a moment, taking in the rising sun.

Felix approached. "You doing okay, Ralph?" he asked.

Ralph smiled. "Actually, I'm doing great," he replied. "Let's go to work, pal."

As he rose from the bench, Ralph looked down at the half medal hanging around his neck and smiled. He knew that no matter how great the distance was between them, Vanellope would always be his best friend.